Simple Lies

Jan Fields

Annie's®
AnniesFiction.com

Library of Congress-in-Publication Data
Simple Lies / by Jan Fields
p. cm.
I. Title
2016935148

AnniesFiction.com
(800) 282-6643
Amish Inn Mysteries™
Series Creator: Shari Lohner
Series Editor: Shari Lohner
Cover Illustrator: Kelley McMorris

10 11 12 13 14 | Printed in China | 9 8 7 6 5 4 3 2

"He who has not Christmas in his heart will never find it under a tree."
–Roy L. Smith

A chilly wind whistled along the sidewalk, prompting busy shoppers to tug coats closer and pull scarves higher. Late December in Pleasant Creek, Indiana, definitely belied the little town's cozy name. Bundled up in a long, navy, wool coat with a tailored Victorian cut, Liz Eckardt was more than used to cold and certainly didn't let it keep her indoors.

She'd lived in Boston and had seen the snow lay so deep on the ground that cars simply disappeared and sidewalk paths were cut almost like tunnels through the snow. Liz wasn't going to be deterred from her Christmas preparations, no matter what Indiana tried to throw at her. She was even hoping for snow on Christmas Eve, but not just yet. Liz didn't want anything to get in the way of her godson's flight home from his military base in Kosovo. Steve had promised he'd have leave for Christmas, and Liz was almost giddy with anticipation.

She hadn't seen Steve since she'd moved to Pleasant Creek and opened the Olde Mansion Inn. When she'd Skyped and emailed with him, he'd been supportive, if a little bewildered. Since Steve had lost his own parents when he was only seven, he could definitely understand Liz's desire to connect with family in Indiana, but the move from busy Boston to the Hoosier state's Amish country was a huge change.

As if in response to her thoughts about the Amish, Liz heard the clopping of hooves on the brick street and turned to watch a black carriage coming toward her. The beautiful sorrel mare pulling the open buggy tossed her head as she passed. Liz felt mild disappointment that she didn't recognize the driver. She got a thrill any time she bumped into her recently discovered Amish relatives. As she watched the buggy, Liz wondered if it would be considered intrusive to drop in on her aunt or cousin, and maybe bring some Christmas presents for the children. She wasn't at all certain what sort of gifts would be acceptable, if any. Did her Amish relatives even exchange gifts at Christmas?

Overwhelmed, she shook off the question for the moment and continued walking. She'd ask Sarah when she got back to the inn. Her young assistant was married to Isaac Borkholder, one of Liz's Amish cousins. The pleasant-natured girl never seemed to grow tired of her employer's questions about their customs.

Liz arrived at Sweet Everything and saw that the bakery was even busier than usual. Pushing the door open, she immediately noticed a change in the sound of the bells over the entrance and looked up with a smile. The bakery's owner, Naomi Mason, had swapped the usual tiny silver bells for sleigh bells. The customary pastel carnations in bud vases on the bakery's white tables were gone as well, replaced by silver tapers in holly candle rings. Red paper place mats added to the festive look of each table. The display cases full of delicious goods were trimmed with narrow pine garland and red velvet bows.

Naomi stood behind the counter, her lovely face as cheerful as ever. She had changed her standard coral apron for a cream one trimmed in festive red and green, which matched the headband that held back her curly dark hair. She waved at Liz before returning her attention to pouring a steaming cup of coffee for a customer.

By the time Liz reached the front of the line, Naomi had Liz's order of gingerbread cookies on the counter. Naomi opened the box to show off the contents. The gingerbread men and women wore crisp outfits of white icing drawn in complex filigree patterns.

Liz gazed at them with admiration. "Oh, those are almost too beautiful to eat."

"You'll change your mind about that when you taste one," Naomi said, her dark eyes sparkling. "I promise your guests will love them."

"I'm sure they will." Liz leaned forward to peer closer at the cookies, breathing in the spicy scent. "Do you think I could run string or ribbon through some of their tops? I've seen gingerbread cookies hung on Christmas trees and they look so beautiful."

"These will be too soft for that," Naomi said. "I could bake a batch that's extra crunchy if you'd like them for ornaments. But, if it were me, I would simply make applesauce dough. It looks a lot like gingerbread and smells wonderful, but it's much more durable. The ornaments will even last more than a year if you store them carefully. Plus, you can use white acrylic paint for the piped icing. It's easy."

Liz gave her friend a wry glance. "Maybe, but I don't know if it would be easy enough. Clearly you've never seen my cookie-decorating skills. Speaking of decorating, I have something else I want to talk to you about." At the sound of shifting feet and rustling gift bags behind her, Liz realized that some of the people standing in line were becoming impatient with her chatting. "But first, you should ring these up before there's an uprising over all the time I'm taking. 'Tis the season to be in a hurry."

Naomi rang up the cookies and then waved one of her staff to the counter so she could sneak away. "I deserve a little break," she said as she slipped into one of the white chairs at a nearby table and rested her forearms on the Christmas place mat. "So let me tell you how to make this applesauce dough." Naomi flipped over the paper mat and began writing ingredients.

"I appreciate it." Liz took a seat across from her friend. "I meant what I said about the decorating, though. Do you think they'll look good without being painted? Maybe I could glue buttons onto them."

Naomi nodded as she finished her list. "Buttons would be cute, but the paint is doable, I promise. I'll even bring my paint over after I close the shop and show you how to do it. You'll surprise yourself. Really."

"I'm ready to be surprised. This is my first Christmas at the inn, and I want everything to be perfect for the guests coming in tomorrow. Plus, my godson is coming home for the holidays. It'll be the first time he's seen the inn." Liz couldn't keep the grin from spreading across her face. "Honestly, I feel like a kid waiting for Santa. This is going to be a fantastic Christmas with Steve here—the best Christmas ever."

"I hope I'll have a chance to meet him."

"I'll make sure you do. But first, I have to finish getting the sitting room decorated before the guests arrive."

"Everyone will be dazzled," Naomi predicted.

"Nice thought, considering that right now I have an undecorated tree, six new guests coming in tomorrow, and a bulldog who, despite resembling a beanbag chair most of the time, still rallied enough to chew the nose off the brand-new Santa I put next to the front door."

"Santa!"

Surprised, Liz turned to see a shocked expression on the face of the woman seated at the next table.

"Surely you aren't decorating with Santa," the lady continued in a tone that sounded as if Liz might be decorating with neon beach balls and paper airplanes.

"Um, no?" Liz said.

"Pleasant Creek is a traditional community," the woman said with a sniff, not seeming the least bit mollified by Liz's response. "We appreciate a spiritual Christmas without all the devious commercialization of *Santa*. That kind of exploitation is ruining our holidays *and* our children!" Apparently so distressed by the idea of a decorative Santa, the woman stood up and stormed out of the bakery.

Liz turned back to Naomi. "Sorry, I didn't mean to drive away a customer"—Liz dropped her voice to a whisper—"with evil Santa."

Naomi waved a hand at the door. "Don't worry about it. She has an opinion on everything and an addiction to my chocolate éclairs. She'll be back." Naomi reached across the table to pat Liz's arm. "And don't worry about Santa either. I doubt one Santa Claus is going to send people running from the inn in horror." Then she added a mischievous smile. "Well, a Santa with a gaping hole instead of a nose in the middle of his face might scare off a few. Your bulldog's handiwork does sound a tiny bit horrifying."

"Thanks, you're lots of help." Liz sighed. "But Santa is only a symptom of my bigger problem. I have no idea how to do a proper Pleasant Creek Christmas, and I have Amish relatives, which means I'm doubly worried. I don't know the traditions or *anything*."

Naomi looked at her in surprise. "But your mom was Amish. What traditions did you have growing up?"

"Our Christmases were simple. Mom generally disapproved of all the commercialization. But we always had a tree, and though I never sat on Santa's lap, she did hang up the ornaments I made at school. I know some of those were Santa-themed."

"So maybe your answer is there—just keep it simple."

"Easier said than done." Liz shrugged. "I don't even know if it's okay for me to bring presents to my cousin's children. And, if so, what kind of presents? I'm assuming no video games."

Naomi chuckled at that. "Probably a safe assumption."

"Sure, *that* assumption's safe, but what about others I might make? I don't want to offend."

"You know, you have two Pleasant Creek experts at the inn all the time," Naomi said. "Just ask Mary Ann or Sadie. They've both lived in Pleasant Creek forever, and you know Sadie will tell you *exactly* what she thinks."

"I do know that," Liz agreed. "But I hate to bother them at the fabric shop. Sew Welcome has been crazy busy with customers rushing in for last-minute holiday purchases. Plus, they have family of their own coming in. Mary Ann's cousin Arthur is staying at the inn right now because her house is overflowing with people. And they're both in that caroling contest. I didn't even know caroling was something you could do competitively."

"That's a lot, but Mary Ann and Sadie have had crazy busy Christmases as long as I've known them. They seem to actually prefer the holidays that way."

"But they canceled a Material Girls meeting," Liz said. "That suggests they're as overwhelmed as I am."

"They didn't so much cancel it as turn it into a cookie swap. You are coming to that, right?"

Liz scoffed. "And have my pitiful cookies compete with yours and Mary Ann's?"

Naomi laughed. "It's not a competition. It's an exchange of baked gifts. And Mary Ann cheats anyway. She makes those tiny tarts and calls them cookies. They are fabulous, though."

"You're not making me feel any better. Besides, having a cookie swap is one more thing for all of us to juggle. I don't want to add to their burden by dumping my Christmas panic on them. And I sometimes worry that poor Sarah is getting tired of all my questions about her new in-laws and their customs. Considering that they're my cousins, you'd think I would know. She never *acts* likes she's annoyed with me, but I worry." Liz rested her head in her hands. "I thought moving to Pleasant Creek from Boston would mean getting away from craziness, holiday or otherwise."

"The whole world gets crazy now and then," Naomi said.

"Excuse me?" A male voice sounded behind them.

Naomi and Liz turned toward a young man who stood shuffling his feet near their table. He had a thatch of dark hair and a hesitant smile. His eyes, behind wire-rimmed glasses, were hard to read. "I don't mean to interrupt, but I couldn't help but overhear your Christmas distress." He set a business card on the table. "My name is Charlie Newman, and

I'm a professional storyteller. I have a whole selection of *Christag* tales, which are full of Amish Christmas customs. Maybe I could help you?"

As he spoke, Liz envisioned a cozy scene in the inn's sitting room, her guests seated about the crackling fireplace, listening raptly to old-timey Christmas stories. "That would be wonderful," she said earnestly. "I own the Olde Mansion Inn. I'm planning to host evening social hours during the holidays with cookies and conversation. A storyteller would be the perfect touch. Do you think you could come and share stories with my guests after dinner one night?"

The young man's hesitant smile bloomed into something so lovely it lit up his dark eyes. "I'm certain I can. Some of the stories are life-changing."

"I'll settle for homey and traditional," Liz said. They quickly worked out the details for the storytelling, and he promised to be at the inn the next night to entertain the new guests. Liz felt part of the burden ease from her shoulders.

Naomi must have noticed the change because she said, "You know, this is exactly the way Pleasant Creek has been for me. When I have a problem, there's always someone ready to help."

Charlie bobbed his head in agreement, his smile wide. "That's *exactly* how this town is meant to be. Exactly!"

By the time Liz left the bakery, she was feeling considerably better. She smiled again at the sound of the sleigh bells chiming behind her as she stepped into the cold. Turning right, she caught sight of a package next to the door. The box was wrapped in brown paper, tied with string, and addressed to Naomi. With the bustle of shoppers on the sidewalk, it didn't seem safe to leave a package outside long; someone could trip over it or step on it. Liz scooped up the package, carefully balanced her cookie box on top of it, and headed back into the bakery.

Naomi was standing at a table, chatting with the two women seated there. She saw Liz and smiled. "Thought of something else you need? More cookies? A cake?"

"No, this time I come bearing gifts, or at least a package. This was outside, in front of the door."

Naomi's smile faded. "That's weird. Packages always come to the back. Even if it was a new driver, you'd think he'd at least bring it inside." She reached for the string-tied box, and Liz managed to transfer the package without dropping it or her cookies, which she considered a pretty impressive feat.

The parcel was about the size of a cake box, and Naomi's name and the address of the bakery were carefully printed on the brown paper wrapping. Naomi turned it over gently in her hands. "Strange," she said. "There are no shipping labels or postmarks at all."

"Maybe it's a present from your secret Santa," Liz teased. Realizing she'd said the S-A-N-T-A word, she flinched and waited for someone else to scold her. Thankfully, no one did.

"Or a secret admirer," one of the women Naomi had been chatting with suggested, leaning forward on her elbows to get a better view of the package. "It's about time a pretty girl like you had a secret admirer." She looked at her companion across the table. "I think it's from the young fellow who owns the bookstore across the street. I've seen him giving Naomi the eye."

Her friend waved off the suggestion. "He'd never get up the nerve to give her anything. I think it's probably Joseph, the builder. I've seen how many brownies he buys in here."

"Psh," the other woman said. "Joseph just likes brownies. Have you seen his middle?"

Liz listened to the exchange in amusement. "Maybe there will be a card inside," she suggested. "Open it."

"Good idea. Plus, I love presents no matter who sent them." Naomi set the box on the table between the two women and carefully took off the brown paper. Underneath was holiday paper with a dark blue background and silver snowflakes. Someone had written on the festively wrapped package in red marker, but apparently decided against the note because it was scribbled out, leaving a blob of red ink behind.

"That has to be from a man," one of the women at the table said. "A woman would have rewrapped it."

"I told you," her companion insisted. "Secret admirer. And Joseph is messy."

Liz had to admit she was getting into the spirit of the mystery and wondered what her friend would find. Naomi gently tore the paper free, uncovering a foam box that resembled a miniature ice chest.

"That's an unusual gift box," Liz observed.

"Maybe it's not a gift." Naomi lifted the lid. A look of disgust crossed her face as the ladies were promptly overwhelmed by a foul odor.

One of the women at the table gagged from the smell, flinging herself away from the table so hard that she stumbled and almost turned over her chair. "Oh, it smells like something died in there!"

Liz covered her nose and looked inside the box where a pile of moldy rags held the body of a dead mouse. Next to the mouse was a single ivory business card, hand-printed with the word *Heartless*.

2

With a strangled gasp, Naomi slammed the lid back onto the box, covering the vile contents. Her skin turned ashen as she stared at the package.

"That was disgusting," Liz said, her eyes fixed on the innocent-looking white foam box. "Who would do something like that?"

"I take back everything I said about the secret admirer," one woman from the table announced as she stood up, holding her nose. "And you'll have to excuse me—I'm going outside for some fresh air." Her companion and most of the people close by followed.

Naomi shook her head. "If this is someone's idea of a joke, it's disgusting." She shuddered. "I'm going out back to get rid of this."

"Don't you think you should call the police?" Liz asked.

"I think the police are busy enough. They don't need to be bothered over a tasteless prank." Naomi walked the package back through the shop with Liz at her heels.

"I still don't know if you should simply throw it away. At least take some photos of the contents and the wrappings," Liz insisted. "I've had clients who were harassed, and it's always better to keep careful records and evidence."

"I'm not being harassed. It's one disgusting box."

"So far."

Naomi turned to push the back door open with her shoulder and gave Liz a frown. "You're cheering me up tons. Thanks."

"I want to be certain you aren't sorry. One disgusting box could turn into more. Every stalker starts with a single act."

"This isn't Boston, and I don't have a stalker," Naomi said as she ducked out the door.

"I still think you need to document it. How could it hurt?"

The icy wind raced down the alley behind the bakery, instantly chilling both women. Liz pulled her wool coat closer around her, but Naomi's sweater clearly offered little protection.

With a shiver, Naomi shoved the box at Liz. "Fine," she said, wrapping her arms around herself as soon as Liz took it. "You can have my evidence. It's too cold out here to argue. But I don't want to see it again, and I don't want to talk to anyone about it. In fact, I'm planning to forget it ever happened." She pulled open the door and went back into the bakery.

Hoping the cold gusts would carry the smell away, Liz opened the box. The wind didn't seem to help much with the stench. She moved her scarf up to cover her nose and mouth, and then took several photos of the mouse and the wrappings with her phone. Next, she took a tissue from her purse and wrapped the business card in it, tucking it into the outside pocket of her bag and hoping it wouldn't bring the package's smell along with it. She also saved the piece of brown paper with the address and the portion of blue paper smeared in red ink. Liz tossed the rest in the trash. She would respect Naomi's wishes and not call the police, but she was reassured to have saved key bits of evidence if needed later.

Liz straightened her coat and readjusted her scarf around her neck. She had to get back to the inn. With a groan, Liz realized she'd left the cookies inside, so she went into the bakery again to retrieve them, stopping along the way to give her hands a thorough wash with hot water and lots of soap.

She exited the front of the shop, carrying her box of gingerbread cookies carefully as she navigated the busy sidewalks. She determinedly put the disgusting package out of her mind and replaced it with a mental list of the rest of the errands she had to do before she could return home.

As she passed each shop, Liz peered at the window displays. Just as the snippy woman in the bakery had claimed, the decorations were traditional with lots of greenery, wooden toys, and candles. The few

Santa decorations she saw wore long robes and beards, and they only appeared in the trendier shops. *Maybe Beans saved me from a major faux pas,* she thought wryly.

Once she got back to the inn, Liz set to work making her applesauce ornaments. She dumped a tall economy container of cinnamon into a bowl, and then added in the other spices from Naomi's list. Finally, she spooned in applesauce and stirred the whole mess into a dough that filled the kitchen with a delicious spicy scent.

The kitchen door opened and Mary Ann Berne walked in, her beautiful silver hair matching the silver threads woven into her midnight blue sweater. The tall, slender woman was followed by her business partner, Sadie Schwarzentruber.

Sadie was Mary Ann's opposite in nearly every way possible. She radiated an earthy good cheer that was both hearty and loud, while Mary Ann had a more peaceful happiness about her. Sadie delighted in telling bad jokes; Mary Ann loved baking pies for everyone she knew. Despite their different personalities, however, they certainly agreed about the importance of good friendships and sewing.

Sadie and Mary Ann were best of friends and co-owners of Sew Welcome, the fabric store that took up a large section of the Olde Mansion Inn's first floor. Popping into the inn's kitchen, they wore their usual smiles. "Something smells interesting," Mary Ann said as she stopped at the table. Then her smile faded. "Did you put that whole container of cinnamon in there?" She turned a concerned face toward Liz. "Are you sure about that?"

"That's too much," Sadie said, and then sneezed from the spice lingering in the air. "I don't think you should serve those cookies. I'm not even sure we should be breathing near them."

Mary Ann nodded, looking pained at the need to be critical. "If you're testing new recipes for the Material Girls cookie swap, I wouldn't use that one." She offered Liz a smile. "I have a very tasty spice cookie recipe I can share."

Liz laughed. "I appreciate that, but this isn't cookie dough. I'm making Christmas ornaments. Naomi told me how."

The expression of relief on Mary Ann's face almost made Liz laugh again. "Oh, they'll be wonderful ornaments," her friend said. "What a clever idea."

Sadie reached into the bowl to poke the dough. "It's a nice color, but the smell is making me hungry for real treats." She chuckled and patted her stomach. "Of course, most things do."

"There's some coffee cake in the bread box." Liz pointed with her elbow while she plopped the dough out on the parchment paper she'd spread on the counter. "But don't dip into the gingerbread men—they're for tomorrow night's cookies-and-conversation time in the sitting room. I've moved the usual afternoon get-together to after dinner for the holidays. You're both welcome to stop by."

"Oh, I will." Sadie peeked into the box on the counter. "These cookies are gorgeous." She looked up at Liz with a grin. "And you know I love conversation. I have some great new jokes I could try out."

Mary Ann shook her head. "If you're talking about the ones you've been telling customers all morning, I'm not sure you can call any of those jokes 'new.'"

Sadie merely laughed at the gentle criticism. "They will be new to Liz's guests."

"You should consider it too, Mary Ann. Coming to the social time, I mean, not regaling us with old jokes. I'm going to have a storyteller," Liz said as she rolled out the dough. "Now all I have to do is get these ornaments done so we aren't gathered around a naked tree."

"I noticed the tree," Sadie said, "but I didn't want to say anything. Don't you have any ornaments or lights? Surely you celebrated Christmas in Boston."

Liz winced. "I had 'designer' trees then, where all the ornaments were funky colors like mauve or metallic teal. I actually gave them to a thrift store before I left Boston because they reminded me of everything

I wanted to put behind me. Besides, those decorations wouldn't fit into the country setting here."

"But you must have some ornaments from when Steve was little and from your own childhood," Mary Ann pressed.

"I do, but I was going to put those on a tiny tree in my room. Most of them are the sort of thing only a mom can properly appreciate." Liz sighed. "I want the inn's tree to be homey and country and perfect. Right now it's just perfectly bare."

"Maybe you should let the guests help you decorate since you're pressed for time," Mary Ann suggested as she snuck a pinch from the coffee cake Sadie had pulled out of the bread box. "They might enjoy that. Tree trimming is lots of fun."

"That could be nice," Liz said as she sorted through her cookie cutters and realized that, aside from a single gingerbread man, they were mostly everyday shapes and animals, not Christmas icons. Maybe Naomi would have ideas about how to make them more festive. She picked out a heart, a pig, and a few other cute ones with no delicate parts that could break off. "Naomi is coming over after the bakery closes to help me decorate these. At least, I hope she is."

"Did she say she was?" Mary Ann asked. "If so, you can count on her. Naomi takes her word seriously."

"Oh, I know," Liz said. "It's just that she had a nasty surprise at work. Someone left her a package with a dead mouse and moldy rags inside. The box was wrapped up like a present, so the awful things inside were quite a shock." She shook her head. "It was horrible."

Sadie wrinkled her nose. "I heard about those."

"Those?" Liz echoed. "You mean someone other than Naomi got one?"

"I know Kinder Clothes did," Mary Ann said. "The owner buys fabric from us for displays, and she was in the shop yesterday. Someone left them a wrapped box full of moldy rags and hay, and a little card that said *Heartless* in handwritten script."

"That's what Naomi's card said too," Liz said.

"That's crazy," Sadie insisted, punctuating her words with thrusts of her fork into the air. "Naomi is one of the sweetest people I know."

"The owner of Kinder Clothes isn't heartless either," Mary Ann said loyally. "She volunteers at the animal shelter, for one thing, and she took part in that big fundraiser for the church last year too."

"Did your friend call the police about the package?" Liz asked. "Naomi flatly refused to. In fact, she would have simply thrown the whole thing away if I hadn't stopped her. I took pictures and kept the card and some samples of the paper."

Sadie raised her eyebrows. "I really doubt anyone has called the police. This isn't Boston. The packages aren't pleasant, but they're hardly something to bother the police about. I imagine this is some kind of prank by teenagers with way too much time on their hands during the winter holidays. After all, hay, rags, and dead mice aren't exactly rare in farm country."

"Maybe," Liz said, but she still thought wrapping up a dead animal was sick, even ominous.

The three women were pressing Liz's cookie cutters into the last of the applesauce dough when Sarah Yoder Borkholder poked her head into the kitchen. The slender young woman wore a dark blue dress that was mostly covered by an apron, and a crisp linen *Kapp* over her fine blond hair.

"Excuse me," Sarah said with her usual soft-spoken formality. "Someone is out in the foyer looking for you, Miss Eckardt. She seems a little impatient."

"I'll be right there."

Sarah nodded and ducked back out while Liz rinsed off her hands.

"I could put the ornaments in the oven for you if you want," Mary Ann said.

"Leave it to us," Sadie added. "And I promise not to sample these particular goods." Mary Ann and Liz chuckled.

"Thank you both." Liz handed the kitchen mitt to Mary Ann and headed for the door. "The oven is already on." She reached the foyer to find a tall, well-dressed woman wearing designer heels and a scowl. The shoes made the woman decidedly taller than Liz, possibly even taller than the Christmas tree. The frowning woman wore her black hair in a sleek twist. She stood with her arms crossed, tapping her foot.

"May I help you?"

"I should hope so," the stranger said, glancing around the room with disdain. "I'm Portia Brecken, and I have a reservation. I am not used to being kept waiting, nor to having to ask the cleaning staff to track down my host."

Liz blinked at the venom pouring off the imposing woman. "Actually, Ms. Brecken, I have you scheduled to arrive tomorrow morning."

"Well, since I'm standing here, that's clearly not right, now is it?" the woman snapped. "I've had a long journey from the East Coast and I got stuck behind one of those ridiculous horse carts outside of town. I had to creep along behind the wretched thing for nearly half a mile before I could pass. I honked but that rude driver wouldn't even pull off the road."

"Well, it is his road too," Liz said, keeping her tone light.

Portia's dark eyes turned sharp and cold. "Paved streets are for *cars*. Those horse-drawn things are a hazard. Aren't there enough dirt roads for them to drive on?"

Liz simply had no idea what to say to that. Why on earth had this woman come to Pleasant Creek? She wondered if it would be possible to pretend there'd been some sort of catastrophe that prevented her from renting rooms to close-minded snobs.

"I want my room *now*," Portia demanded.

Luckily Liz saw Sarah lurking in the archway that led to the fabric shop, and she gave the girl a desperate look. "Sarah, is the Somewhere in Time Room ready?"

"Yes, ma'am, it is. I finished making up the bed a short while ago. I'd be happy to show your guest to her room."

I couldn't do that to you, Liz thought. "That's all right, Sarah. I'll escort Ms. Brecken." She forced a smile and said to the grumpy guest, "If you'll follow me, please."

Portia peered down her nose at Liz, using her extra height to emphasize her superiority. "You can't imagine I'm going to carry my own bag."

Liz wondered what she could possibly have done to deserve a Christmas guest like this one. Her smile began to ache as she said, "No problem, I can carry it." She hefted the massive suitcase and led the obnoxious woman upstairs.

Liz felt lucky to reach the door to the Somewhere in Time Room before the heavy bag wrenched her arm out at the shoulder. She threw open the door and waited for the quirky room to work its magic on the rude new guest. As always, the beautiful old pine floor glowed, and the furniture wore not one speck of dust. Sarah was an obsessive cleaner. Wall clocks, shelf clocks, and mantel clocks filled the room, though most didn't run since the ticking could be annoying to lodgers. Still, the clock faces always seemed friendly to Liz.

If Portia was charmed, she didn't show it. Instead, she sniffed. "I suppose one can't expect much this far out in the boonies."

"I hope you will enjoy your stay," Liz said through gritted teeth. "You'll find a brochure on the side table with a list of local events." She went on to give her standard description of breakfast and the social hour, though she knew her tone lacked its usual sincerity.

She was relieved when Portia practically shoved her out of the room. Liz had no more interest in being there than Portia had in talking to her. With luck, the dreadful woman would shun all company until it was time for her to check out. That would be a true Christmas gift.

Liz headed down the stairs, rushing to get back to the ornament project before Mary Ann and Sadie did all the work. She hoped the new folks arriving in the morning would have more of a traditional holiday spirit, or a perfect Christmas might be difficult to come by.

She reached the bottom of the stairs, but before she could turn toward the kitchen, the front door swung open. For a moment, Liz wondered if it was later than she thought and Naomi had arrived. Instead, she spotted the last person she'd ever expected—or wanted—to see again.

Oh no, she thought. *No, no, no, no, no!*

3

The man standing in the doorway with an overnight bag slung over one shoulder had the kind of chiseled good looks that belonged on magazine covers, not lurking in Liz's inn on a day that was already taxing her Christmas spirit to the max. The chill outside had brought a flush to his cheeks, and he held a present wrapped in beautiful gold paper with a red bow. His artfully mussed hair and insincerely shy smile made Liz want to smack him for the liar she knew he was. The man was her ex, Matt Sheridan. And everywhere that Matt went, pain was sure to follow. Liz most certainly didn't want any more of it landing on her.

"There's my girl," Matt said, crossing the space between them swiftly and handing her the present. He leaned in to kiss her lips, but Liz ducked quickly and he made contact with her forehead instead of his intended target.

She shoved the gift back at him. "What are you doing here, Matt?"

"Can't a guy visit his best girl at Christmas?"

"I'm not your girl—best, worst, or otherwise," Liz said, backing away until she nearly tripped over Beans, who was, unsurprisingly, sleeping heavily on his favorite rug. "Why is the concept of *ex* so baffling to you? I thought you got the message the last time you popped up at my inn."

"You thought that was me giving up?" He chuckled and smiled at her fondly, as if her desire to be rid of him was simply adorable. "I only backed off to give you time to realize you're a Boston girl, not a country mouse."

At the word *mouse,* Liz's gaze sharpened as she remembered Naomi's disgusting package. Right now, she'd consider an expired rodent pleasant company compared to her smooth-talking, delusional ex. "I'm very happy where I am."

"You say that, but I know you. You thrive on the pressures of city life and the courtroom. You were one of the best patent attorneys in one of the most exciting cities in the country. How can cleaning toilets in Indiana compare to that?" He edged closer. "Boston is beautiful right now, babe. It's snowing. I remember how gorgeous you look with snowflakes on your lashes, sparkling like jewels."

Impervious to his flattery, Liz folded her arms over her chest. "I'm not having this discussion."

Matt gave her his full wattage smile. "You know I could change your mind if you'd give me half a chance, and I'm going to stay right here until you do."

"Oh no you're not. You are *not* staying in my inn."

"It's a public inn, isn't it? And I'm part of the public." He looked around the scrupulously clean foyer. "It's not up to my usual standards, but I don't mind slumming for you. It's a far cry from that fantastic ski resort we stayed at last year on the day after my grandfather's holiday party. Remember that?"

"Again, I am not having this conversation, and you are not staying in my inn." She looked him up and down with a frown. "I know what part of the public you really are—the disreputable part."

He took another step closer to her, and she took another step back. Liz felt a brush against the back of her legs and glanced down. Apparently her increased volume had managed to rouse Beans from his nap. The bulldog had waddled closer and was now leaning heavily against her leg and glaring up at Matt.

"I see you still have that mutt," Matt said, scowling back at the dog. "As if you needed something else to bring down the class of this place. That thing is just ugly."

"Looks aren't everything. You taught me that."

He grinned again, wider this time. "That sounds like a compliment."

"Then you misheard." Liz shifted slightly to relieve the mass of the dog against her leg, resisting the urge to wince. It was hard to appear tough with a hefty English bulldog crushing her ankle.

Liz almost gasped with relief when Beans got up and shuffled toward Matt. The dog growled deep in his barrel chest.

Matt backed away toward the front door, clearly remembering his last encounter with Beans, which hadn't resulted in anything resembling friendship. "You need to tie up that crazy animal!"

"I don't think so," Liz said. "This is his home, and I *like* him, which is something I cannot say about you." Of course, Beans sometimes drove her crazy as well, but at least he had an excuse for acting like a dog.

"If he bites my ankle and ruins these brand-new boots, I'll sue you!"

"Go ahead. Like you said, I'm an excellent attorney," Liz countered. "You can always leave. You're close enough to the door."

"What's going on down here?" Portia stood near the base of the stairs, her imperious voice ringing out in the foyer. "I cannot believe you allow that creature to harass your guests."

"This guy isn't a guest."

"I am too," Matt said uneasily from his position against the door. "I want to check in, the same as anyone else."

Portia walked closer. "Why on earth would you choose to stay here with that beast?"

Beans turned his attention to Portia, apparently suspecting she was insulting him. He stared at the snooty woman but didn't growl, for which Liz was grateful. She supposed it wasn't exactly professional to have the dog attacking Matt in the foyer.

"Beans," she called, patting her leg.

Beans gazed at Liz for a moment. He apparently decided guard-dogging was too much work, because he waddled back over to his rug and flopped down with a huff.

"There, Beans isn't threatening anyone," Liz declared.

Matt stepped away from the door and pasted on his signature smile. "Great, so I can check in."

"No. You cannot."

"Is the inn full?" Matt asked.

"No, but I have more guests coming in tomorrow. And you definitely do not have a reservation."

"Will the inn be full when your guests arrive tomorrow?"

"Full enough."

"What kind of inn is this that you try to talk people out of staying?" Portia interjected. "Someone told me this place was lovely, but I think she must have meant loony."

Liz suddenly had a mental image of a horrible online review—the kind that multiplied as it got picked up by every travel website in cyberspace. She suspected Portia was exactly the sort to do something like that. "Matt isn't a normal guest."

"Is it your place to judge your guests?" Portia pointed her alarmingly hawklike nose at Liz and scowled. "Is this a professional establishment or is it not? I was hoping for a suitable place to spend Christmas."

"This is a professional establishment, but—"

"Then I certainly hope you're going to give that poor man a room."

Liz tried to argue awhile longer, but somehow she found herself agreeing in the end. She wasn't certain how it happened or why Portia cared so much about where Matt would sleep, but at least she was able to stick Matt up on the third floor, though the beautiful Sunset Room was entirely too nice for him. Matt would have to share a bathroom with Mary Ann's cousin Arthur. She hoped Arthur was a total bathroom hog.

Not wanting to endure any more of her ex's efforts to charm her, Liz sent him off with Sarah to get settled in his room.

Finally she was alone in the lobby with Portia. "I'm sorry," Liz said, making an effort to smile. "Things usually run much smoother around here. Did you need something?"

The haughty woman looked down at Liz. "I wanted to tell you that I will not be joining your little chitchat event tonight."

"Thank you for letting me know," Liz said, her mood brightening as Portia sauntered off. At least that was one nice thing. Now all she had to do was avoid contact with Matt and get her Christmas ornaments done before tomorrow's guests arrived. She headed for the kitchen, and when she opened the door, the heady scent of apples and cinnamon wafted out.

Mary Ann stood at the counter gently transferring baked ornaments onto a cooling rack with a spatula. "You didn't tell me how long to bake them," she told Liz. "But I thought it was probably good to overbake them a little so they'd be hard."

"Good thinking." Liz smiled appreciatively. "I didn't mean to stick you with this chore."

"I don't mind. You know how much I love baking, and the smell does remind me a little of apple pie. Sadie had to go back to the shop, though. We've been so busy that we couldn't both be gone long."

"I'm surprised the excitement in the lobby didn't draw her out." Liz poked one of the warm ornaments gently. "I know how she enjoys a good brouhaha."

"She must have had a customer," Mary Ann guessed as she pulled another pan of ornaments from the oven. "Nothing else could have kept her away. What happened?"

"You remember Matt Sheridan?"

"That handsome guy with the bad manners? Yes." Mary Ann's eyes widened. "Don't tell me he's here."

Liz nodded. "And somehow I've rented him a room." When Mary Ann's expression turned even more surprised, Liz held up a hand. "Please don't ask. I certainly didn't want to. It just sort of happened; there was a witness. I'm trying to block out the whole experience from my mind."

"Well, I'm sure you handled it with aplomb," Mary Ann said. "Now, if you don't need me, I'm going to go help Sadie close up for the day. Then I'm bringing Arthur home to have supper with all the relatives staying at my house—a group that seems to change a little every day."

"Sounds chaotic and wonderful," Liz said, and she bid her friend a good evening. Liz had never experienced the joy of a large family, though meeting some of her Amish relatives in Pleasant Creek had helped a little.

She carefully transferred the rest of the ornaments from the cookie sheet to the wire rack and made herself a soothing cup of tea. She could certainly use it.

While Liz was sipping her drink, Sarah came in. "I've gotten Mr. Sheridan settled and finished up for the day," the girl announced. "I thought I'd be going, if you don't need me for the social hour?"

"I won't be having a social hour today. Ms. Brecken isn't interested, and Mary Ann is taking her cousin home for dinner, so we have no guests to socialize with."

"What about Mr. Sheridan?"

Liz shuddered. "I hope he skips it as well." Then she had an idea. "Could you do me one more favor before you leave?"

"Of course."

Liz pulled a slip of paper from the notepad that she used for grocery lists and quickly wrote a message for Matt. She told him the social hour was canceled and reminded him that as a guest of the Olde Mansion Inn he was welcome downstairs, but Beans had the run of the first floor. *Hopefully that will keep him upstairs*, she thought, handing the note to Sarah with a request for her to slip it under Matt's door. Sarah left the kitchen to deliver the message, and Liz returned to her tea.

After the stresses of the day, Liz lost herself in thought for a while. She sat on the stool with the mug between her hands, staring off into the distance as time passed. She was shaken out of her reverie when she heard a knock on the kitchen door.

Naomi poked her head in. "Anyone home?"

"Oh, Naomi. I lost track of time." Liz hopped off the stool to greet her friend. "I'm sorry."

"No problem. As you can see, I let myself in." Naomi walked to the counter and examined the racks of cooled ornaments. "Oh, these came out nicely. None cracked?"

Liz shook her head. "No, but I don't think I can take credit for the good result. Mary Ann helped, and you know she works magic in the kitchen."

"That she does—especially with her pies. I like to think of myself as an impressive baker, but if she challenged me to a pie bake-off, I'd go ahead and concede defeat." Naomi lifted a heart-shaped ornament and sniffed it. "These are going to make your sitting room smell yummy."

"As long as Beans doesn't try to eat one."

"He'd probably regret that. They wouldn't taste very good."

"He ate Santa's plastic nose. I can't imagine that was exactly lip-smacking."

Naomi laughed. "I guess it wasn't so bad to a dog." She began unloading tubes of white paint, plastic sandwich bags and brushes from her purse. "Let's get to work decorating these not-so-tasty treats."

Naomi squirted a big glob of paint into a plastic bag and poked a tiny hole in the corner. Then she squeezed the paint out of the bag and onto an ornament in a neat line. "It's exactly the same as decorating a cookie."

"That's what I was afraid of." Liz gamely prepped her own bag and managed to pipe a simple face on a traditional gingerbread-man shape. She peered at it closely and thought the little guy looked less than cheery. "I think he's as worried about Christmas as I am." Then she told the tale of her ex's arrival.

"Wow." Naomi glanced up from the neat mustache she was putting on her own applesauce-dough man. "And I thought my day was rough."

Instantly remembering what had happened to her friend that day, Liz replied, "I suppose Matt isn't quite as bad as a dead rodent. It's pretty close, but I think you had the most revolting surprise today."

"What did you do with that thing anyway?"

Liz looked at her friend in mock innocence. "He's up on the third floor."

Naomi chuckled. "No, the mouse, silly. I hope you didn't keep it."

"I tossed it in the trash. I took its picture though."

"Oh, don't let Rob Carver hear that you have photographs," Naomi warned as she finished the little dough man and moved on to a pig.

"Rob Carver?"

"He's a reporter at the *Pleasant Creek News & Views.* You don't recognize the name?"

Liz gave her a sheepish smile. "I have to admit I don't read the local paper, not since seeing a lost cow on the front page once."

"Now that's simply city snobbery," Naomi teased, gesturing at Liz with the end of her paint bag. "Lula is a very important cow. She's the mascot for the Sweet Lula Dairy, and she's on all of their television ads. Plus, she sometimes leads the harvest parade and takes part in ribbon cuttings. You should ask the mayor about her. I understand they're very close."

"I can't believe I've missed meeting such a notable Pleasant Creek celebrity all this time," Liz said dryly. "So back to Rob. I assume the guy upset you?"

"Poor Rob." Naomi finished piping some delicate filigree on her pig cookie. "He wants to be a big-city reporter, and he's certain that he'll hit pay dirt eventually—some big scoop that goes viral and gets him out of Pleasant Creek. I honestly believe he'll invent a story if he doesn't find one soon."

"Why would he have to invent something with a rich topic like Lula around?"

Naomi wrinkled her nose at Liz. "You stop picking on Lula."

Liz raised her hands in surrender. "Fine."

"At any rate, I think Rob is seeing some crazy mystery where none exists."

"Maybe," Liz said, not wanting to annoy Naomi as she had at the bakery. "Though you're not the only one who has gotten one of those nasty packages. I mentioned it to Mary Ann and Sadie, and they told me Kinder Clothes got a box too."

Naomi set her pig aside with a sigh. "I know. Rob was all too happy to tell me that Cracked Pots got one as well. He's absolutely certain this is the beginning of something huge and sinister."

"Cracked Pots?" Liz asked, not recognizing the shop name.

"It's the little artisan gallery at the edge of town. You haven't been there?"

Liz shook her head.

"You should go. They have so much local work, and it's amazing."

"And they got a package? So there are three businesses that have been targeted."

"That we know of." Naomi shrugged. "I suppose there could be more. I know I wouldn't have advertised getting one of those awful things if I'd had the choice. A dead mouse doesn't really draw people to a bakery. And now Rob is going to make a big deal out of it in the newspaper, because that's what he does. This is a busy time of year for me, and I don't need people driving out of town for their holiday baked goods."

Liz set down the slightly deranged-looking dog ornament she'd been decorating. "No one is going to abandon Sweet Everything over this. Certainly not anyone who has ever tasted your baking."

Naomi gave her a quick hug. "You're such a good friend."

After that, conversation turned to more pleasant things, including Liz's excitement about her godson's visit, and the two women finished painting designs onto the rest of the applesauce-dough ornaments. Liz thought her decorating improved near the end, but her creations still paled in comparison to Naomi's works of art. As Liz examined the pan full of gorgeous ornaments her friend had painted, she didn't think Naomi needed to worry about anyone avoiding her bakery.

———————— ∕∕∕∕∕∕∕∕∕∕∕∕∕∕∕∕∕∕∕∕∕∕∕ ————————

The next day began early, as the days always did. One thing Liz had learned as an innkeeper was the value of being a morning person. She walked through the utility room to the side door and let Beans out for his morning constitutional before she got started on breakfast. For Beans, outdoor exercise usually amounted to sniffing the shrubs closest to the door and flopping down about five feet away for a snooze on sunny days. In the cold of December, he was less enthusiastic, doing his business quickly and practically running Liz over to get back inside. But even Beans could be full of surprises now and then.

"Hurry, please," Liz said as she watched Beans slowly waddle outside and sniff the air. She wrapped her arms around herself to ward off the chill.

Beans didn't even give her a glance. Instead he inhaled again and suddenly bolted, racing around the building as fast as his stumpy legs would carry him.

"Beans!" Liz shouted, shocked to see that he could move so fast. "Come back here!" She ran after him, assuming he wouldn't get far before flopping down to snort and wheeze. Of course, that would probably mean she'd have to carry him back into the house. *And I'd hoped this was going to be a better day than yesterday.*

As Liz made the turn to the front of the inn, she saw Beans near the porch steps, attacking a box covered in brown paper. "Beans! No!"

With more than a little effort, Liz got the package away from the bulldog, but not before he'd ripped off a corner of the brown wrapping to reveal another layer underneath. A feeling of dread settled in the pit of her stomach as Liz realized that she recognized the design—it was the exact same bright blue holiday paper she had seen just yesterday at Naomi's bakery.

4

Beans flopped down on the cold ground as Liz very carefully turned the box over in her hands to scrutinize it. The Olde Mansion Inn's address was neatly penned on the outside, in handwriting identical to the careful writing on Naomi's package. If the box had ever had a return address, that part was presently in the belly of a grumbling bulldog.

"Come on," she called to Beans. "I'd better find out what's inside this thing."

She walked back around to the side of the inn with the bulldog more or less at her heels and carried the package into the utility room. She considered the worn but clean table that ran along one wall and decided she didn't want her special delivery on it. She hated the idea of dumping something gruesome out of the box onto anything in the house, even a work surface. She swallowed down a nervous lump, hoping a dead mouse was the worst thing she might find inside.

Liz stopped near the table. She removed the rest of the brown paper and the blue layer and then opened the box with it still in the crook of her arm. To her relief, the signature ivory business card lay on top of a pile of rags with no dead animals in sight. As with Naomi's "present," the card read *Heartless*. Was that what the mysterious prankster was calling himself? Or was it some kind of indictment of the person receiving the gift? If so, that didn't make any sense at all. Naomi was anything but heartless, and Liz hoped that no one in town thought she was heartless either.

As she hesitantly poked around in the box, Beans must have caught the scent of the half-rotten shreds of fabric because he managed another unexpected burst of energy and lunged against Liz's legs, making her stumble. She dropped the box on the utility table, scattering most of the contents—rags, bits of hay, several tiny teeth, and an old bone.

Liz stared in horror at the mess. Though she was far from an expert, the bone looked a lot like a human finger bone. *Why oh why couldn't it just have been a mouse?*

As she gaped at the bone and teeth, Liz realized she had no choice. She had to call the police. Whatever was going on, it certainly seemed to go beyond some bored teenager's prank. Liz phoned the police department and explained about the package.

"You too?" the woman on the other end of the line responded. "Can't the kids around here just play with their cell phones when they're bored like everyone else?"

"Have you seen these things?" Liz asked. "I'm not sure this is a kid's prank."

"I haven't seen one myself, but I've heard about them. Rags and business cards? That doesn't seem all that scary to me."

"Tell me that when you find one on your front step. At any rate, I'd like someone to come out and take a look at this, please."

"No problem. We've got a rookie who could use some practice." The woman ended the call before Liz could voice her sarcastic thanks for relegating her concerns to a training exercise.

Liz paced back and forth in the utility room as she waited for the police and wondered why anyone would send her such a gruesome package. She supposed it was possible she could have offended a few people in the community, but not this badly. And she'd certainly never had any kind of hostile interaction with teenagers in town.

When a light tap sounded at the side door, Liz rushed to answer. A clean-shaven young police officer with a blond buzz cut stood outside. "You wanted to report an offensive package, ma'am?"

Liz let him in and gestured across the utility room to where she had left the box and its contents. "Apparently there's a rash of these around town. I don't know how many of the other shop owners have called about them."

He shrugged slightly. "Fewer than you'd think, but word gets around." He crossed the room to peer down at the tiny pile of teeth and the single bone resting on the utility table. "I hadn't heard about any others with human remains though." He turned to give her a wry smile. "Apparently you're special."

"That kind of special I could live without. I had sort of expected Officer Dixon to handle this. He's been here before."

The young policeman's smile widened. "So I've heard. But Officer Dixon isn't on duty today."

She heard another tap at the side door and gave the police officer a questioning look.

"My partner," he explained. "Actually my training officer. I'm new."

Liz opened the door again, and this time the policeman outside was closer to her age, with thinning hair and a belly that overhung his pants. He tipped his hat to Liz. "Ma'am. I'm Officer Hughes." His gaze swept by her, and he added, "You've met my partner."

"Right," she said as she stepped to one side. "Though I didn't get his name."

The younger police officer flushed. "I forgot. I'm Jack Gerst."

Officer Hughes grinned at him. "You forgot you're Jack Gerst? That doesn't sound too good. I thought it was just us old guys who forgot our names."

The younger officer's cheeks pinked even more. Then he straightened his shoulders, taking on a more serious air. "You ought to take a look at these, George."

Officer Hughes winked at Liz as he walked to the table and scrutinized the debris from the package. "Somebody sure has a sick sense of humor." He looked up at Liz. "I didn't see any sign of stray tracks outside, but the ground is pretty hard this time of year. Have you seen any strangers around?"

Liz offered him a weak smile. "I'm still fairly new to the area, and I own an inn. I see strangers on a daily basis."

The older policeman nodded. "Fair point. Have you had any altercations with one of these strangers?"

"Not really."

"What's going on in here?" The deep male voice that called out from the hall was all too familiar, and Liz groaned as she turned around.

"This is nothing to concern you, Matt." She hurried over to block his way into the long, skinny room.

"I'm a guest here, so I think it does concern me." Matt leaned sideways to look around Liz at the utility table. "Is this some kind of weird Amish custom—sending rotten rags at Christmas?"

"Hardly," Officer Gerst said as his eyes zeroed in critically on Matt.

Matt folded his arms and leaned against the doorframe with one ankle crossed over the other. It was the kind of pose you might see in a movie or a magazine, but not something people actually *did*. "I don't know, Lizzie. This seems to be one creepy place you've picked for a new home. It's rather troubling, really. Isn't this the second time you've had to call the police here?"

Liz had no intention of discussing how many times she'd had to summon the police, especially since she'd have to correct him with a higher number. She admitted to herself that Pleasant Creek could certainly be more exciting than she'd expected, and sometimes more dangerous as well. To Matt, however, she would admit nothing. She glared at him, trying to come up with something that would get him out of the utility room.

Beans had been watching the two police officers with about as much interest as the bulldog normally showed, meaning he'd flopped under the utility table and kept an eye on them with as little movement as possible. But apparently Matt warranted something a little more physical. The stout bulldog hefted himself to his feet and lumbered across the room like a wheezing freight engine. He skidded to a stop next to Liz and growled, the sound rumbling deep in his chest.

Matt immediately took a step back. "You keep that mutt away from me."

"He's simply protecting me," Liz said amiably. "He must think you're some kind of threat. You know what they say about dogs—they're a much better judge of character than people are."

Matt pointed at her. "This inn doesn't stand a chance as long as you give that vicious creature the run of the place."

"Funny," she said. "He doesn't seem vicious to anyone else." She turned to the police officers. "Does he seem vicious to you?"

The young officer looked down at the stout dog, whose chest still rumbled with growls directed at Matt. "He certainly didn't act viciously toward *me*." He looked intently at Matt. "Were you outside this morning, perhaps in front of the inn?"

Matt opened his mouth to respond to Gerst's obvious suspicions, but at that moment Beans ramped up his growling and took one step forward. Matt ducked out of the doorway, retreating across the short hallway. "I've been inside all morning!" he called from the safety of the kitchen.

Liz sighed with relief. Getting Matt out of her hair should make the day easier.

As she bent to pat Beans on the head, she heard another knock at the side door, this one insistent. Liz traded looks with the policemen, who both shrugged.

"Not one of ours," Officer Hughes said.

Well, it can't be Matt, so how bad can it be?

A moment later, Liz silently reminded herself to stop tempting fate as the tall, slender man in the doorway introduced himself as Rob Carver. With his red hair and freckles, he looked like a grown-up Huckleberry Finn. "I work for the *Pleasant Creek News & Views*. I'm the lead reporter on the mysterious packages story."

Liz nearly groaned at that. She rather doubted the small local paper had a team of reporters covering a creepy prank, which meant the young reporter was inflating his importance. "Yes. I've heard of you."

The reporter's face brightened, making him look even younger. "Really? Great. I want to ask you some questions about the package you received and maybe take a few photos." He held up a camera.

"What makes you think I received a package?"

His smiled widened still further. "I have a police radio." He leaned around her and waved. "Hi, George."

The older officer nodded agreeably, but his young partner gave the reporter a disapproving scowl.

The reporter tried to step around Liz. She put a hand on his chest to halt his progress, but he still managed to edge part of the way into the room.

"What do *you* know about these packages?" she demanded.

Rob gave her a long, considering look, but relented. "No one knows much. They seem to be mostly rags and hay, though they stink to high heaven. But the bakery got a box with a dead animal in it, so things are starting to get juicy. I don't suppose you got a dead cat or the severed head of a horse—something interesting like that?"

Liz cringed at the thought. "That's disgusting."

"It's news," he said, trying once more to step around Liz.

Again she blocked his way. Liz wondered if it would be possible to get Rob out of the room and the door closed without shoving him. The utility room was freezing with the draft coming in from outside, and her patience was wearing thin.

Rob's cocky smile turned into a pout. "Aw, come on, I've got a job to do. Let me look."

"I have a job to do too," Liz said. "And it doesn't involve encouraging lurid stories about my inn."

The reporter stood on tiptoes and took a photo over her shoulder. "Hey, George, are those teeth I see? Do you think this is going to turn into a murder investigation?"

The older policeman gave the reporter a disgusted look. "I'd better not see any speculation about murder in the paper. No murder investigation here." He pointed at the teeth. "None of these have roots. They're some kid's baby teeth."

The reporter's eyes widened. "Someone is pulling out children's teeth?"

"No, I expect they fell out on their own," Officer Hughes said. "Or did you not hear the part about no roots?"

As annoyed as Liz was by the reporter, she was deeply relieved to hear that the policeman didn't think they were looking at foul play. "Are you certain?" she asked.

The officer nodded. "I've got experience with baby teeth. My two kids both insisted those things were worth two dollars apiece when they stuffed them under their pillows. I remember getting a quarter when I was a kid and being glad of it."

"Fine, the teeth fell out on their own," the reporter conceded, using the distraction to duck around Liz and wedge himself into the utility room. "But I saw a bone too. No kid is losing bones and sticking them under a pillow."

"It's just one bone," Officer Hughes countered. "And we have no evidence that it's human. It could be a chicken bone for all I can tell. The only obvious thing is that it's pretty old. You can call the station later, Rob, and if the chief wants to give a statement, he'll give you one. Until then, wild speculation doesn't help anyone."

Resigned to the fact that Rob wasn't going anywhere, Liz closed the door and looked at the pile of debris again as the younger officer delicately swept bits into evidence envelopes. "So you don't think that could be a finger bone?" she prompted.

Officer Hughes shrugged. "Hard to say." His impassive expression broke into a smirk. "You know, the guys down at the station have been commenting on how much more . . . interesting Pleasant Creek has become since you came to town."

The reporter perked up at that. "In what way?"

Liz ignored him. "You can't blame *me* for this rash of disgusting packages. I wasn't the first victim, or even the second for that matter. I'm at least the fourth that I know of, so this definitely isn't my fault."

"We're not blaming you, ma'am," Officer Gerst said quickly, giving his partner a disapproving look.

If the older man was at all chagrined by his young partner's silent reprimand, he didn't show it. Instead, Hughes asked Liz a few questions about how she found the package while Gerst finished packing up the evidence. With every answer Liz gave, she saw the reporter scribbling frantically.

When Officer Gerst picked up the handwritten card with a pair of tweezers to drop it in an evidence bag, his training officer pointed at the card with the end of his ink pen. "Do you know why someone might call you heartless, Ms. Eckardt?"

Liz shook her head. "I like to think I'm not heartless, but I also don't think the card is about me personally. It looks identical to the card that was in Naomi's box."

"You were there too?" Officer Hughes asked. "At the bakery? Do you have a connection with any of the other recipients?"

"Naomi is my friend. I only saw her package because I was there picking up cookies. She didn't want to call the police over something that she thought was probably a prank. But I hated to see all the evidence end up in the dump, so I took photos and saved the card."

"Could you get it for us, please?" Turning to the younger policeman, Officer Hughes added, "Be sure to bag this with a separate label."

Liz fetched the card and samples of paper from her purse in the kitchen. After Officer Gerst bagged the paper samples, the older policeman held up the two *Heartless* cards side by side

"They sure look the same," Officer Hughes said.

"You can tell they're handwritten." The reporter stepped closer to gesture toward the cards. "See the difference in width on the flourishes? And they were written by the same person." He turned to look at Liz with one eyebrow raised. "A person who is not a fan of yours."

Liz chose not to respond to that. The police officers finished up their work and left with the evidence. The reporter tried to linger behind, but Liz pushed him out the side door. As a business owner, she didn't want to alienate anyone from the newspaper, but there were limits.

With no time for a sigh of relief, she rushed into the kitchen to get back to work.

Sarah peeked into the room and asked, "Do you need my help with breakfast?"

Liz glanced at the clock and yelped. "Yes, desperately. But first, could you sanitize the table in the utility room? I can't imagine ever being comfortable touching it again after what was just on it." She waited for Sarah to ask her for details, but she'd underestimated the girl's respect for Liz's privacy.

"I'll get it clean," Sarah assured her. "Are you sure you don't need help with breakfast first?"

Liz grabbed eggs, milk, and a bowl of chopped veggies from the fridge. "I'm fine. A nice frittata should be quick to put together." She carried the food to the counter and began breaking eggs into one of her big mixing bowls. As Sarah started toward the hallway, Liz called, "Did you see anyone in the dining room?"

"Not yet, but I did hear your . . . friend ranting about a dog in the kitchen. He said he'd never eat anything cooked around all that dog hair."

Liz paused in her egg beating to look down at the floor where Beans was sprawled as flat as one chubby bulldog could possibly manage. "Matt has a lot of faith in dog hair's ability to fly."

Sarah snuck her a sideways glance. "He seems like someone who enjoys complaining," she ventured quietly.

"Only when he's not getting his way," Liz said, dumping handfuls of chopped vegetables into the egg mixture. "At least the new guests haven't arrived yet."

"No ma'am. Though the fancy-dressed lady heard all the talk about the dog, and she said she refuses to eat any of the inn's food either."

"That should make breakfast easier." With both of her more obnoxious guests boycotting the morning meal, Liz only needed to feed Arthur. The prospect of having leftover frittata for lunch brought a smile to her face.

The rest of the morning kept Liz on the run doing normal inn chores. With the lunch hour creeping closer, she decided to ask Sadie and Mary Ann to join her for leftovers in the kitchen.

As she opened the door to Sew Welcome, she heard a familiar, unwanted male voice talking to someone inside. " . . . I am amazed you even want to have a shop in this place, especially with some stalker leaving boxes of dead animals and human body parts all over. Who knows what will turn up next? Maybe a dead body? After all, it wouldn't be your first murder around here, would it?"

5

Intending to give Matt a piece of her mind, Liz was nearly through the sewing shop door when she heard Mary Ann's quiet voice informing him that he clearly didn't understand Pleasant Creek or Liz very well. Then Sadie demanded he buy something or get out of the store. Liz had just enough time to duck out of sight as Matt steamed by. She watched him with a smile. It was nice to see someone else tell off her ex for a change.

Mary Ann and Sadie seemed delighted to join Liz for lunch and were unusually complimentary about the frittata.

"I remember when the only way I ever cooked eggs was scrambling," Sadie said. "My husband wouldn't touch anything but the basics, so I scrambled a lot of eggs over the years." She held up her fork. "This is a real treat."

"Thank you," Liz said wryly. "Though it's a treat you've had quite a few times now."

Sadie gave her a sheepish grin. "Okay, fine. I was trying to cheer you up after your morning."

"You both already cheered me up when you tossed Matt out of your shop."

"Your ex is a real pain," Sadie said.

Liz winced at Sadie's blunt but accurate assessment. "I only wish he'd take his ex status more seriously."

Mary Ann reached across the table to pat Liz's hand. "We can't blame him for wanting to be around you. But if you avoid him as much as possible, I expect he'll get the message and move on."

"Wouldn't that be a nice Christmas present?" Sadie crowed.

After lunch was cleared away and Liz's kitchen was again sparkling, the day's expected guests began to arrive. The first to bustle through the front door were elderly twins Gina Fritz and Lois Granger, both dragging wheeled luggage behind them. The two women peered up at Liz with matching brown eyes behind thick glasses. Although not identical, they each had a fuzzy puff of white curls poking out from under handknit caps.

After Liz welcomed them, the sisters examined the foyer cheerfully. "This is going to be perfect," Gina said as she tugged off a pair of mittens that matched her hat. "A real country Christmas." She gestured toward the candles and greenery in the windows near the front door. "I love all the homey holiday touches."

"Thank you. I hope you'll enjoy your stay." Liz was suddenly anxious about showing the women the sitting room where the tree remained glaringly bare, which didn't seem like the sort of homey holiday touch they had in mind. At least she'd gotten rid of the mangled Santa.

"We will," Lois said, turning a fond gaze toward her sister. "We always do. Every year, Gina and I have a get-together in Indiana, because it's halfway between where I live in Maine and where she lives in Texas. But we decided not to stay in Indianapolis this time."

"Too commercial," Gina explained.

Lois nodded. "Far too commercial. We wanted some simplicity this year, and we felt an inn in Amish country would offer that. And we've already seen buggies!"

"And beautiful horses," Gina said. "I don't suppose they ever put sleigh bells on the horses?"

"Not usually," Liz said. "The Amish don't believe in drawing a lot of attention that way."

Gina clapped her hands. "Of course. See what we mean? Simple. Exactly what we wanted."

"I do try to keep things simple," Liz said. *Not that I manage to do it that often.*

"Excellent!" the sisters said in unison. They looked at each other and tittered.

When Liz led the ladies into the beautiful Rose of Sharon Room, they cooed over the white vintage furniture and feminine floral quilts.

Lois opened the door of the tall French armoire and turned to grin at Liz. "I don't suppose I could talk you into selling me this piece and shipping it to Maine. It would be perfect in my bedroom."

"If I did that, where would my guests put their clothes?" Liz asked. "But I am glad you admire it too. It's one of my favorite pieces."

Once she settled the friendly sisters into their room, Liz headed back downstairs to find two more guests had arrived—Judy and Jerry Shelton, a handsome couple who looked to be in their sixties. Liz enjoyed the way the silver-haired man doted on his wife.

"This is our second honeymoon," he announced. "We had a Christmas wedding thirty years ago, right here in Pleasant Creek. It was the perfect spot to start a life with the perfect wife."

Mrs. Shelton gave him a fond smile and patted him on the arm. "He'll talk your ear off about it if you let him. Your inn is lovely."

"Thank you." Liz looked closer at the fragile-looking woman and wondered if they'd had a hard trip. Mrs. Shelton was pale with dark circles under her eyes.

Liz showed them to the Heirloom Room so they could settle in and rest. The room seemed a fitting choice for a second honeymoon, as it sometimes acted as the inn's bridal suite. Liz always found the white-and-blue color scheme soothing and hoped Mrs. Shelton would as well.

Mr. Shelton quickly hustled his wife over to the cushy contemporary sofa, where she sat and gazed around the room.

"Your decorating is lovely," Mrs. Shelton said. "This is such a peaceful room."

"Thank you, though I can't take credit for my favorite part of this room, the white carved fireplace. It was here when I bought the inn."

Mrs. Shelton nodded and clasped her hands in her lap. "It is beautiful. We're going to be very comfortable here, I'm sure. I'm so glad we came."

Liz told the couple about the inn's breakfast, as well as the evening social in the sitting room. "Tonight, we're going to have a storyteller share some Christmas tales."

Mrs. Shelton turned to her husband. "Won't that be wonderful? I love storytellers."

"I'm sure it will. You'll have to rest so you feel up to it."

Liz wrapped up with the couple and headed back downstairs. She only had one more scheduled check-in left, and she was happy that today's new guests seemed to be far less trouble than the ones who'd showed up the day before. She crossed her fingers, hoping that the last guest would be pleasant.

Though Liz didn't exactly believe in the power of finger crossing, she was relieved to find the next arrival, Vivian Whittson, was just as delighted to be there as the others had been that day.

The young woman exuded excitement at spending Christmas in the middle of Amish country. "I've been looking forward to this all year," she said as she climbed the stairs to the second floor behind Liz. "I saw two different Amish buggies when I drove through town. We certainly don't have those in Chicago! And the shops—even from the car I could tell you have some adorable shops. I hope I can pick up some authentic Amish handicrafts while I'm here."

"Of course." Liz snagged one of the local attractions pamphlets from the hall table on the second floor. She pointed out several Pleasant Creek businesses listed in the pamphlet to Vivian. "I don't know if you're interested in furniture, but Cross Furniture Company employs a number of Amish men. They produce amazing pieces with hand tools."

Vivian clapped her hands. "That's exactly what I'm looking for. Do they ship?"

Liz nodded as they reached the door to the Amish Room. "To Chicago, yes. I'm not sure about farther afield."

Entering the room, Vivian squealed with pleasure over the massive walnut bed that featured a benchlike love seat attached to its footboard.

The quilt that covered the bed was appliquéd with silhouettes of Amish figures and scenes against blue, gold, and dark red backgrounds. "It's perfect, totally perfect."

Liz sighed with relief. Things were definitely looking up. She trotted down the stairs, headed into her private room, and made straight for her computer. She was still waiting to hear when Steve would land stateside, and it was hard not to check her email constantly. To her delight, she spotted Steve's username in her inbox.

Liz eagerly clicked on the email. She couldn't wait for him to arrive and promised herself that she wouldn't let the bustle of innkeeping prevent them from sitting down for some nice cozy chats. She also made a mental note to keep Steve and Matt as far apart as possible if her ex was still around. Her godson had never cared for the slick reporter, and she doubted he'd feel any fonder now that she and Matt were broken up.

Liz's cheerful anticipation and mental planning shrank into a cold, hard ball in her stomach as she read Steve's email, and she struggled to fight tears so she could read all the way to the end. Filled with apology and regret, the note said that Steve was not going to be able to get to Pleasant Creek for Christmas after all.

. . . Sometimes duty and the service ask a lot from us. And I especially hate that I can't even tell you details of what has come up. But don't worry about me, Mom. I'm not in any danger, only sad that I won't be spending Christmas with you.

Steve ended his message with a promise to visit for at least a week in January. Liz tried to find that uplifting, but her spirits had sunk too low. She barely noticed that she'd closed the email program and walked back out of her room, through the kitchen, and out past the entrance to Sew Welcome until Mary Ann's gentle voice startled her.

"Liz, what's wrong?"

Liz wiped at her teary eyes with the back of one hand. "I heard from Steve. He won't be home for Christmas after all." She choked up on the last two words, but fought through the lump in her throat to add, "He has some kind of mission."

"I'm so very sorry." Mary Ann hurried over to give Liz a hug.

After a lifetime in Boston, Liz was still a little startled when someone offered her an unsolicited hug, and it took all her willpower not to collapse onto her friend and sob loudly.

"What's going on out here?" Sadie asked, joining the other ladies.

Liz took a step away from Mary Ann only to discover she was too emotional to speak.

Mary Ann rescued her by saying, "It was bad news from her son. He won't be home for Christmas."

"I'm sorry to hear that," Sadie said, her normally boisterous volume dampened. "I know you were so looking forward to his visit. Did he tell you why?"

Liz shook her head. "He couldn't say. He said he'll be home in January."

"I hope that trip doesn't get canceled too," Sadie said.

Liz's eyes widened; she hadn't considered that. A sob rose up in her throat, and she swallowed it down. "You'll have to excuse me." Her voice sounded hoarse. "I need to do something in the kitchen." As she rushed away, she heard Mary Ann scolding Sadie for giving Liz something new to worry about.

For the next couple of hours, Liz threw herself into work to keep her mind off her sadness. She scrubbed her already-clean kitchen and threaded red ribbons through her applesauce-dough ornaments, but she found that looking at the sweet, rustic trimmings only added to her gloom. She even hooked a leash to Beans and tried to drag the reluctant bulldog for a short walk around the yard. She finally gave in when she realized she was ruining the poor dog's day as thoroughly as Steve's email had ruined hers.

Liz trudged back into the kitchen and began altering her meal plans for the coming days. She'd included all of Steve's favorites, and she just didn't have the heart to fix the dishes without her godson around to enjoy them. As she crossed out items and penciled in possible alternatives, it dawned on Liz that she'd need a new grocery list. Then she realized that the alternatives she had come up with all sounded dull and awful. Surely the guests deserved better than that. Suddenly the task seemed overwhelming and Liz's feelings broke through, leaving her sobbing with her face in her hands.

She couldn't believe Steve wasn't coming home. She'd been looking forward to his visit so much, wanting him to see her new inn. She'd even pictured him lounging in one of the cozy chairs next to the personal tree in her private quarters, opening her gifts for him on Christmas morning. At the thought of the stack of neatly wrapped presents she had piled in her quarters that wouldn't be opened on Christmas Day, she erupted into fresh tears.

When Liz finally felt cried out, she snatched a tissue from a nearby box and blew her nose loudly.

"Liz, are you all right?" a deep voice asked from behind her.

Startled, she spun to face Jackson Cross, the mayor of Pleasant Creek and owner of Cross Furniture. As always, Jackson was the definition of ruggedly handsome in his white wool sweater and dark pants.

I must look like a swollen-eyed, red-nosed mess. Liz hurriedly swiped at her face with the tissue, hoping beyond hope that she'd at least be spared the horror of having a runny nose in front of him. "I'm fine. I had some disappointing news today, that's all."

"I'm sorry to hear that." Jackson's hazel eyes filled with kindness. "Do you want to talk about it? I'm a pretty good listener, or so people tell me."

Liz shook her head but still told him her troubles. "My godson won't be home for Christmas."

"Your godson? The one in the military? I hope he's all right."

"He's fine. And I'll see him in January. It'll be okay. I'm just feeling a little disappointed." She sighed. "Actually, a lot disappointed."

Jackson continued to study her face, making Liz even more self-conscious about what she could only imagine was a frightful sight. Finally he nodded. "Quite a lot, I think. It must be rough. I'm sorry to barge in. Sarah told me you were in the kitchen."

"That's all right." Liz smiled, hoping it didn't look too ghastly. "Excuse me for running on about my problems. Did you need something?"

"I do, but I hate to bother you when you're obviously having a tough time."

"Bother me, please. I need something to take my mind off feeling sorry for myself."

"I might have just the thing." Jackson held up one of the *Heartless* business cards. "I'm collecting information about the mysterious packages that have been appearing at different businesses. Cross Furniture Company got ours this morning. I don't like what I'm hearing about them popping up all over town."

"Oh no," Liz said. "Did your package have teeth and bones too?"

"Teeth?" Jackson casually closed the distance between them and leaned against the counter beside her. Liz found the handsome mayor's proximity somewhat disconcerting. He lacked the movie-star suaveness and charm that Matt pulled off so effortlessly, but Jackson's good looks and genuine concern for others was a distracting combination in itself.

"My package had baby teeth," she managed to say, pulling her attention away from his firm jaw and compassionate eyes.

Jackson frowned. "No teeth in the one I found this morning. It had more of the rags everyone seems to be getting and some bones."

"Human bones?"

"I'm fairly certain they were animal bones, though I couldn't tell you what kind. Something with a tail, I believe."

"Charming." Liz dried the last of her tears and threw her tissue in the trash. "Someone sure knows how to send festive gifts. Did you call the police?"

"Yes, I told them this is getting out of hand. Chief Houghton is apparently operating on the prank theory. He didn't seem very worried about it when I spoke with him." In the warmth of the kitchen, Jackson shoved up the sleeves on his sweater, derailing Liz again with his strong forearms.

"They sent the chief of police to investigate Cross Furniture's package?" Liz asked. "That must mean they're taking it more seriously than I thought."

Jackson smiled ruefully. "Actually, I think it just means I'm the mayor. But they did promise to find out what type of bones were in the box, and I got a list of the businesses who called the police over the packages."

"Not everyone has called. I think some of the businesses don't want that kind of public attention. They figure it's a prank and toss the box."

"I know. In fact, I've been wondering about one group that definitely wouldn't call the police over something like this."

"The Amish."

Jackson nodded. "They prefer not to get the police involved in minor matters. I've been asking around, but I haven't been able to find out if any of the Amish-owned businesses have gotten a box. No one will talk about it. Even the men who work for me are being tight-lipped, and I consider them friends."

"Why wouldn't they tell *you?*"

"Because it's not their way to gossip with the English," Jackson said. "And no matter how long I live here or how many jobs I offer, I'll always be an outsider. I'm not family." Then he smiled. "But *you* are."

"Me?" The statement caught Liz off-guard. "I'm still 'that lawyer from Boston' to half the people in this town."

"But not to your cousin Miriam. Not after all you did for Isaac."

After Miriam Borkholder's son had been accused of murder, Liz had helped to uncover the truth. She'd won the undying gratitude of both Miriam and Sarah, who had married Isaac after his name was cleared. "My cousin and I are growing close, but it's still a little shaky. I'm not Amish and that's not going to change. I don't think Miriam is going to be any more open to confiding in me than you."

"Maybe, but I'd appreciate it if you'd go out to the Borkholder farm with me while I ask about the packages," Jackson said. "The contents seem to be growing more gruesome with each delivery, and I don't buy the whole prank theory. I'm worried about what this might spiral into. If this is affecting everyone, I don't want the Amish isolated from the solution. They're as much a part of Pleasant Creek as anyone."

"I'll come with you, of course. I just don't want you to get your hopes up. And I'll have to be back in time for our evening social. I have new guests."

Jackson visibly relaxed when she agreed to accompany him. "I promise to get you home on time."

They walked to the front of the inn so Liz could tell Sarah that she was leaving and pass the word to Mary Ann and Sadie as well. She found Sarah coming downstairs with a slip of paper in her hand and a concerned look on her face.

"Miss Eckardt, the gentleman insisted I give this to you immediately."

Liz groaned, suspecting which "gentleman" Sarah meant given the distress on her face. "I hope he wasn't rude to you."

"The English have their ways," Sarah said softly, clearly echoing something she'd heard before.

"Matt's ways are especially annoying." Liz unfolded the note to find that Matt was demanding a meeting to talk with her, specifically without her "attack dog" or any of the "nosy old ladies" around. He warned that if she didn't see him, he'd write a review of the Olde Mansion Inn so scathing that it would keep guests away for years. Liz crumpled up the paper angrily. She didn't need more trouble, but she hated to give in to Matt's blackmail.

"Is something wrong?" Jackson asked.

Liz shoved the crumpled note into her pocket. "It's something I'll need to deal with later." She turned to Sarah. "I'm going out with Mr. Cross for a while. If the 'gentleman' bothers you again, tell him I'll speak to him when I return."

Matt might be able to force a meeting, but he couldn't force her to make it a priority.

6

The drive out to the Borkholder farm was pleasant, though less picturesque and somehow lonelier with the bare trees reaching for the gray sky with twisted, skeletal limbs. The fields no longer held waving rows of tall corn. Instead, they were littered with broken and trampled stalks, waiting through the winter for a fresh spring planting.

Cows still stood in some of the fields, looking plump in their thick winter coats. Steam rose from their nostrils as they snorted into the chilled air and watched Jackson's truck pass. As always, Liz enjoyed the signs of how far removed she was from her past life in busy Boston.

Like the fields, the flower gardens that normally brightened the Borkholder yard with color were sleeping through the winter. The only sign of life was a holly bush with glossy leaves and bright berries planted at one corner of the yard.

As Jackson's tires crunched over the gravel drive, the sound drew Miriam Borkholder out onto the porch of the big white house, and she raised her hand in greeting. The rockers that normally graced the porch were gone, stored for the winter.

"What a wonderful surprise," Miriam said as Jackson and Liz approached her. "I have been wanting to get into town to invite you for a visit, but Christag preparations have kept me busy."

"I can imagine so." Liz accepted her cousin's hands in greeting. Liz knew the Amish woman wouldn't be so effusive as to hug her, but Miriam grasped her hands firmly and held them for a long moment. "I hate to admit my ignorance, but I wasn't certain whether it would be acceptable for me to visit over the holidays.

My mother's diary said Christmas Day involves prayer, fasting, and reading Scripture."

"You are correct that the day itself is a time of thoughtful appreciation," Miriam said with a smile. "But one of the things we appreciate is family. Christag is a time for family to come together. You are family. And I happen to know that Keturah is making you a gift."

Tears suddenly touched Liz's eyes as she felt a wave of tenderness at her cousin's simple kindness.

If Miriam noticed Liz's rush of emotion, she didn't draw attention to it. "It is always good to see you as well, Mr. Cross. Will you both come in?"

The house was so clean that it looked like something from a magazine. To Liz's surprise, Grace and Keturah sat at the long table skillfully weaving a wreath from fir branches. Both girls wore blue dresses and long black stockings. They gave Liz shy smiles before ducking their eyes when they saw Jackson behind her.

"I didn't know you made wreaths," Liz said to Miriam.

"It is a nice change of pace from the quilting. The girls help me of course. We sell most of them in town for some extra money to buy a few gifts. We keep Christag simple, but I enjoy working with the greens. It brings such a nice smell to the house and helps me miss my flower gardens less. The boys make stars from cut branches, though they work out in the barn. As always, we keep busy."

"Stars?" Liz echoed. "I thought your elder didn't approve of stars."

"He does not like to see them on our barns and in our homes, but he does approve of being industrious. The stars sell well in the Pleasant Creek shops. We do not use them in our home, but I would not judge those who do."

"Not even those with big Christmas trees?" Jackson asked.

Keturah laughed aloud at that, but quickly covered her mouth and dropped her gaze back to her wreath. Grace gave her younger sister a mildly disapproving look, but didn't speak.

"We have seen the big trees in town," Miriam explained. "Keturah is amused at the idea of bringing a whole tree into one's home. And she finds it even more entertaining when the tree is made from plastic and wire."

Keturah aimed her wide gap-toothed grin at Liz and bobbed her head in agreement. Her older sister still looked mildly scandalized.

Liz knew the Amish believed in moderation in all things, including temperament, and she hoped that Keturah wasn't scolded too often for her lively nature. She was glad to see Miriam look fondly at her daughter.

"We do not have Christmas trees," Miriam continued. "But we get together with family and exchange gifts." She turned her smile toward Liz. "And now you are part of our family. I hope you will come to join us for dinner the day after Christag. That is traditionally the time to get together with our friends and extended family."

"I would enjoy that very much." Not only was Liz touched to be included in the Borkholders' holiday plans, but she was also relieved to have an answer for her question about exchanging presents with her Amish family. Her mind was already buzzing with simple but thoughtful gift ideas for her relatives.

"I hope you can bring Steve. I have looked forward to meeting him after hearing you speak of him so many times."

At the sound of her godson's name, Liz felt a fresh pang of hurt. "That won't be possible. Steve can't come home for Christmas. I heard from him today."

Miriam's usually serene expression darkened, and she reached out to squeeze Liz's hand. "I am sorry to hear that. It is difficult news this time of year."

Liz nodded, fighting back tears at her dear cousin's kindness. Jackson rescued her by stepping forward. "I'm sorry to intrude, but I have a question to ask you, Miriam. It's about packages that have been left at businesses in Pleasant Creek."

Miriam's face grew closed, and she spoke to Jackson softly. "I have not been often to town these last weeks."

"I realize you probably aren't privy to information about things left at non-Amish businesses. But I do wonder if any of the Amish families or businesses have received mysterious packages of rags and hay."

"My family has received nothing like that. I cannot speak for anyone else in the community. It is not our way to talk about our neighbors." Miriam didn't add anything about not speaking with the English in particular, but Liz could hear it in her tone.

Jackson looked at Miriam quietly for a moment before continuing. "I want to stop whoever is delivering these packages. They're upsetting, and I'm concerned about how far this person might go to be disruptive. I would like to figure out who's doing it soon, before anyone gets hurt."

Miriam nodded, her indigo eyes still troubled. "I understand, but I can say nothing to help you."

Though they spoke for several more minutes, the conversation remained stiff. Liz felt bad about coming out with Jackson and hoped it wouldn't affect her relationship with Miriam. Her cousin was so warm and kind, but Liz's ignorance of the Amish customs meant she constantly worried about accidentally offending her new family.

Finally, as they wrapped up and Jackson led Liz out onto the porch, Miriam repeated her invitation to dinner after Christag, and Liz felt a bit better.

When the front door closed behind them, Jackson put a hand under Liz's elbow to guide her gently toward the truck. "I'm sorry," he said. "I know that was awkward."

"A little. I only hope Miriam isn't mad at me."

Jackson smiled. "The Amish around here are amazingly

forgiving. This certainly isn't the first time I've given unintended offense, though I always try to navigate the waters carefully."

They were nearly to the truck when the door to the house flew open and Keturah ran across the porch, her bonnet askew and her braids flying behind her. "Cousin!" she called. She then seemed to remember that running wasn't permitted, and she slowed to a fast walk. "I want to show you something."

Liz beamed at the little girl. "You must show me quickly. It's too cold to be outside without your coat."

"I'm not cold," Keturah declared. She stopped and held up a slip of linen. "I wanted you to see the present I made for *Mutter*. It's a bookmark for her Bible."

Liz looked at the carefully hemmed cloth. "That is beautiful stitching," she said, knowing it must be difficult for the active little girl to be still long enough to do such work.

"I knew you would like it. I showed it to Grace, but she reminded me not to be proud." The little girl sighed. "It is hard not to be proud sometimes."

"I imagine it is."

"I knew you would understand." Keturah leaned closer to Liz and spoke in a hushed tone. "I have heard about those packages you were talking about with Mutter. Someone left them in two different buggies."

Liz looked at Jackson, who raised his eyebrows but didn't speak, letting Liz handle the girl. "Do you know which families?"

Keturah nodded enthusiastically, but before she could continue, they heard Miriam call the child's name. All three looked up to see Miriam walking out onto the porch wearing a long wool cloak. "Come in the house before you catch cold. It is not seemly to test *Gött* by going outside without your coat."

"Goodbye, Cousin," Keturah said, giving Liz's hand a quick squeeze before sprinting back to the house, gaining another mild scolding for running.

Miriam closed the door her daughter had left standing open and walked toward Liz and Jackson. "Keturah likes you. She speaks of you often."

"I like her too. She's so full of life."

Miriam smiled. "She is certainly that." At the sound of an approaching buggy, she said, "That will be Philip. Will you wait for a moment? He would be glad of the opportunity to greet you both."

"Of course," Liz agreed, though she still felt a little nervous around Miriam's taciturn husband. Their relationship had been rocky at the beginning due to the trouble Isaac had innocently found himself in and Liz's connection to the situation, but Philip had warmed to his wife's cousin over time. Still, his precise politeness never softened into anything Liz might call friendliness. She had to remind herself constantly that the Amish were a reserved people.

A beautiful horse, its coat shining in the winter sun, pulled the black buggy into the drive. Philip brought the buggy to a halt and climbed down from the driver's seat, handing the reins over to a muscular young man Liz readily recognized, not the least because his high cheekbones, full mouth, and coloring mirrored his mother's.

Liz raised her hand in greeting. "Hello, Isaac."

"Greetings, Cousin." Sarah's husband nodded at her and turned the buggy toward the barn.

Philip's long-legged stride allowed him to cover the distance to Jackson, Liz, and Miriam quickly, though he showed no sign of hurrying. He looked down at Liz, his eyes kind. "It is good to see you. I trust you have had a good visit with Miriam."

Liz smiled. "Always."

Philip raised his eyes to Jackson and offered his hand, which the mayor shook heartily. "Welcome, Jackson. This is unexpected."

With their broad, muscular builds and rugged features, the two men looked enough alike to be relatives, though Liz much preferred Jackson's open, easy personality.

"Philip, I'm looking into some unwanted packages that have been left at businesses around Pleasant Creek," Jackson said.

"Packages?" Philip repeated, his expression turning wary.

"Boxes filled with rags and hay, some with animal bones and things like that. I want to put a stop to them before they lead to something even more unpleasant—and possibly dangerous." Jackson gazed at Philip evenly. "I know some Amish have gotten the packages as well."

Philip glanced at Miriam, and she gave him an almost imperceptible shake of the head. "I have not received such a package. Even if I had, we prefer to deal with problems of the community within the community. You know that is our way, Jackson."

"I understand that. But this problem seems to be crossing into both worlds here. And as mayor, I care about all the people of Pleasant Creek."

Philip looked again at Liz, his face solemn. "Are you here on Jackson's errand or your own?"

"I'm always happy to see Miriam and you," Liz said. "But I came out with Jackson because the packages worry me. I got one. It was disgusting, filled with rotten rags and human teeth and some kind of bone."

Philip's face darkened. "I am surprised to hear that these parcels have gone to others outside of the order. We had believed this was something only our people were receiving. Sometimes people assume that the simple life we choose and our adherence to a moderate lifestyle in all things means we are cold. The *Heartless* cards found in these boxes seemed to suggest that belief. The packages have been upsetting to our community." He paused for a moment, clearly deciding something. "I will speak to my neighbors and learn who has received these parcels and tell you. But we will not speak with the police about it. That is not our way, especially not for something that is probably an attempt to get attention."

"Are the packages always left in buggies?" Liz asked. "Or has anyone discovered one at their doorstep? That's how mine was left. My dog sniffed it out on the porch. And I found the one at the bakery outside the front door."

"No one has mentioned finding one at their home," Philip said, "only in buggies when they are left tied up on the streets in town."

"That's odd," Jackson said. "Perhaps whoever is leaving them isn't willing to come so far out of town. Thank you for telling me what you know. I appreciate your trust."

Philip's smile, though mostly hidden behind his beard, warmed his eyes. "You are an old friend of our community, Jackson, and Liz is family." His words surprised Liz. She knew Miriam loved and accepted her as family, but Philip, with his quiet reserve, was so much harder to read.

After a few more minutes of conversation about the winter weather and the farm, Liz and Jackson headed back into town. They rode mostly in silence, both deep in their own thoughts. Liz realized that helping Jackson learn more about the mysterious packages had lightened her gloom over Steve and his call to duty somewhat, though she was still painfully disappointed that she wouldn't see her godson for Christmas. He would have loved having an Amish Christag meal with Miriam, Philip, and their children. Though Liz knew the Amish were all committed pacifists, she was certain they would still show Steve the same warmth they offered her. Liz sighed. She'd wanted to give Steve the same joy at having new family for Christmas that she had felt herself.

"Thinking about your godson?" Jackson asked, glancing her way.

"Yes, but I promise not to burst into tears."

"I wouldn't think poorly of you if you did. Christmas can be wonderful, but it can also be hard. We have so many hopes for an idyllic holiday, but life rarely delivers on the fantasy."

"That sounds a tiny bit cynical."

Jackson shook his head. "Not really. I love Christmas and having time with family and friends. But I try to be flexible and work around the inevitable catastrophes to enjoy what I do have."

"Good philosophy," Liz said. "And one I will try to embrace because my guests certainly don't want to see me moping around during their stay. Not that I expect to see that much of them. Pleasant Creek has so many things people can do during this time—Christmas concerts and nativity plays and the parade. That parade certainly has odd timing, by the way."

"You mean because it's on Christmas Eve?"

"Yes. I would think people are pretty busy on Christmas Eve."

"True, but the light parade is a Pleasant Creek tradition. All the folks taking part in the caroling competition walk with candles as they sing. The crowd sings along too. And then there are the floats . . ."

"Floats?" Liz pictured the elaborate floats she'd seen the one time she'd gone to the big Thanksgiving parade in New York City. "In Pleasant Creek?"

Jackson laughed. "It helps if you define the word *float* loosely. Many of the local businesses string lights on trucks or classic cars, and put homemade displays in the truck beds or on hay wagons they pull with their tractors"

Liz was tickled by the idea. "Does Cross Furniture do a float?"

"I'm afraid not. As mayor, I usually ride in Joe Holtsclaw's 1961 Chevy Corvette convertible. I wave a light stick at the crowd and pray that I make it to the end without frostbite. They tried to talk me into wearing felt reindeer antlers once, but I knew I had to draw the line somewhere."

"Sounds delightful. Are you doing that this year?"

Jackson braked gently at a stop sign. Cows in a nearby fence ambled closer to the truck as Jackson waited for a slow-moving tractor to cross the intersection. "Not this year. Joe's car is in the shop, so I'm going to be an observer."

"No one else has a convertible?"

"They're all in use for our other dignitaries, like city councilmen and the Pleasant Creek corn queen."

"And the cow?"

"Cow?"

"Lula," Liz said with a grin. "I heard you two were close."

Jackson chuckled heartily at that. "I didn't realize you knew about Lula. Yes, she and I have met many times, but she doesn't join in for the Christmas parade. I think the lights scare her." He glanced at Liz again before advancing through the stop sign. "So, do you want to go?"

"To the parade? You make it sound so appealing."

"It is fun, actually. And I can pack a thermos of hot chocolate to keep us from freezing solid."

Liz gaped at him. "You're inviting me to go with you?"

He laughed. "Don't look so surprised. The mayor is allowed to do something fun once in a while. And if you come with me, I can help you plan a float for the Olde Mansion Inn next year." He grinned at her. "I know a guy who would loan you a nice pickup. I might even be able to find you a cow."

"How could I possibly say no?"

When they reached the inn, Jackson hopped out to open Liz's door. "I hope you won't mind if I don't walk you to the door. I want to go by the police station and talk to the chief. I'll give you a call afterward to let you know what I find out."

"I'll find my way just fine. Thanks," Liz said. "For everything." She turned and hurried toward the front door, feeling much lighter than she had when she'd left. She hunched up her shoulders against the wind and stuffed her hands in her pockets.

The sound of Matt's note crinkling under her fingers sank

Liz's spirits like a rock. *I suppose now I have to go find out what he wants.* One thing she knew for certain—she wasn't going to enjoy another chat with her ex.

7

The trip up the stairs to the third floor of the inn had never felt as long as it did when Liz went to find Matt. Even the gleaming wood floors on each landing and the silky feeling of the polished stair rail under her hand didn't fill her with the usual warmth at being the owner of such a beautiful place. She'd put a lot of work into the inn, but it was all invisible to her as she trudged up the stairs, rehearsing arguments in her mind that would keep Matt from giving the Olde Mansion Inn the terrible review he'd threatened.

She was so caught up in her imaginary discussion that she didn't see the woman on the third-floor landing until she'd nearly run into her. The surprise on Portia's face mirrored what Liz felt. "Ms. Brecken? Can I help you?"

The haughty woman drew herself together and her open mouth snapped closed. Then she looked down her nose at Liz from the lofty heights of her spiked heels. "I wondered if the accommodations on this floor were any better than the rustic hostel room you stuck me in." Her gaze swept over the beautiful ivory pitcher full of holly boughs that sat on a delicate cherry table nearby. "I see they are not."

Since the Somewhere in Time Room that Liz had given the dreadful woman was anything but rustic, she felt a fresh rush of annoyance. "I'm sorry your room isn't to your liking," she said through teeth clenched into a painful smile. "I could call around and find you a place at another inn, if you wish."

Portia's lips twisted into a sneer. "Relocating would be one more inconvenience, and how much better could any other place here in the boondocks be? I will simply make do." She stepped around Liz and tromped down the stairs.

Liz watched her for a moment, fighting the urge to wish the woman a sprained ankle on account of the ridiculous shoes she wore—shoes Liz herself would have worn back in her lawyer days. *I'm so glad I got out of that world.*

Taking a deep breath to strengthen her resolve, Liz marched over to Matt's door and rapped on it smartly. The door flew open, but Matt looked surprised to see her, though his startled expression was quickly replaced by a smirk.

"I wondered if you were ever going to stop by. Come in." He stepped back from the door and gestured into the room with a flourish.

"I would have preferred not to stop by," Liz said. She didn't step into the room. "Surely whatever conversation you have in mind can be had out here in the hall."

"You weren't so standoffish in the past, as I recall."

"I'm smarter now." Liz gestured toward the landing. "We can talk here."

Matt shrugged and stepped precisely into the space she'd indicated. He shoved his hands into the pockets of his charcoal slacks and rocked on the balls of his feet. "I have an invitation to extend."

She raised an eyebrow. "An invitation to what?"

"The Sheridan family Christmas dinner. My grandfather specifically asked for you to attend. You know he adores you."

For a moment, a smile pulled at the corner of Liz's pursed lips. She loved Matt's family and missed them terribly. In fact, to be perfectly honest, they were the reason she'd stayed with him as long as she had. While Matt's charm was fake and self-serving, theirs was gracious and generous. Despite the family's considerable wealth, they never made Liz feel inadequate. In that family, Matt wasn't just the black sheep—he was more like a stray goat that had wandered into the flock and began butting heads.

Since her breakup with Matt, Liz had considered calling his sister once or twice, especially when decorating the inn; Cordelia Sheridan had incredible taste. But Liz hadn't wanted to give Matt any wrong ideas. Plus, she didn't quite know how to bridge the gap back to his family, as her relationship with Matt had not ended amicably.

"Wouldn't it seem strange for me to attend that party," she asked, "considering we aren't dating anymore?"

"Details, details. They wouldn't mind. We wouldn't even have to talk to each other much. You know my family would monopolize your time since it's been so long since they've spoken with you. You could simply enjoy being with them and pretend I wasn't there at all."

Liz narrowed her eyes, wishing he wasn't *here* at all. "And what would you get out of my attending?"

His smile widened. "Hope. I thought perhaps returning to Boston for a reminder of how civilized people live would snap you out of this ridiculous idea of innkeeping in the backwoods of Indiana."

"Pleasant Creek isn't the backwoods." Liz was indignant. "And I have no interest in moving back to Boston. This is a much better fit for me."

He snorted. "That's absurd. You're an educated woman, a lawyer! Tell me, who in Boston would consider dead animals and old bones a gift? You've fallen into a horror movie here."

"That's a little melodramatic."

"You think so?" Matt raised his eyebrows until they touched the thatch of hair that fell over his brow, a look she'd once found endearing. "Anyone who would give dead animals and bones as a present would probably also hurt someone, or worse, kill someone. They're *deranged.* Come on, Liz, I'm worried about you. You need to come back to Boston, at least until the country cops catch this guy."

"I'm not scared, and I'm not going to be driven out of my home. Not by a few sick pranks, and not by you."

"You should be scared," he snapped. "What will it take for you to come to your senses?"

Suddenly a dark suspicion struck her. Could Matt be leaving the packages around town in an attempt to scare her out of Pleasant Creek and back to Boston? Liz hated to think he'd do something that sick, and drag innocent people into it as well, but she suspected there wasn't much he wouldn't do if properly provoked. But why?

"You're putting a lot of effort into this," she said.

"Because it's important to me. I haven't been able to get you out of my head since you left me. I *dream* about you, Liz. We were great together, and I don't know how you can walk away from that. Come back with me for Christmas and give me another chance. Give your old life, your real life, another chance."

"So you've been in Boston pining away for me?"

"You find that hard to believe?"

"Very. Come on, Matt, the only thing that our breakup hurt was your ego. You haven't been pining for me. I'm not ever getting back together with you. Not ever as in *never*. I don't know the real reason you're here, but I do know that it's not because you're lovelorn. Go home to Boston. This is my home now, and I'm staying." She pointed an accusing finger at him. "And I'd better not find out you're the one behind those disgusting packages."

"Me?" Matt yelped, the surprise on his face looking remarkably genuine. "I'm wounded that you'd even think that of me. I would never do anything that low."

"I hope not. I truly hope not. Now I have preparations for tonight to handle, so you'll excuse me, I'm sure." Liz turned and headed back down the steps, the image of his gaping mouth lingering in her mind as she went.

When she reached the kitchen, she found the room was already bustling with activity as Sarah and Mary Ann stood shoulder to shoulder, carefully laying the gingerbread cookies from Naomi's bakery on doily-lined china plates for the gathering in the sitting room.

Mary Ann looked up and smiled as Liz walked through the kitchen door. "I didn't mean to take over," she said. "But Sarah was concerned that you might not get back in time to do the setup."

Liz noticed Sarah's fretful expression, and she smiled at the young woman. "I'm so sorry I made you worry, Sarah. Thank you both." She looked down at the cookies. "These look great."

"Having eaten Naomi's cookies many times, I don't doubt that they *are* great," Mary Ann said. Then she glanced sidelong at Liz. "Which reminds me—you do remember the cookie swap for the Material Girls is the afternoon before Christmas Eve?"

Liz's shoulders slumped. "I'm supposed to compete with you and Naomi in cookie baking?" She pointed at the delicate filigree frosting on a gingerbread pony. "That hardly seems fair when you see something like this, does it?"

Mary Ann shook her head. "It's not a competition. It's sharing. And I seem to remember that you make wonderful oatmeal-macadamia nut cookies."

"I bought the frozen dough for those," Liz confessed. "All I did was put them in the oven and take them out before they burned. As I recall, the cookie swap is supposed to be for actual homemade treats."

"Oh. Well, your chocolate chip cookies were fantastic too."

"Same company. They make excellent dough."

Sarah watched the two women quietly, and then said, "You made nutty fudge bars once from scratch. I saw you."

Liz nodded. "I did. That was a recipe I found online. Those were good."

"See? You have the perfect contribution," Mary Ann said as she carefully wiped a few stray crumbs from the counter into her hand and dumped them in the nearby sink. "So you'll be at the cookie swap, and everyone will love your nutty fudge bars." Before Liz could respond, Mary Ann picked up a cookie platter. "I'll help carry these to the sitting room."

Liz turned to Sarah. "Could you grab that other tray? I want to bring the applesauce-dough ornaments. I thought the guests could help trim the tree while we nibble cookies."

Sarah picked up the plate and gave Liz a shy, encouraging smile. "They will enjoy that." Then a small frown line appeared between her eyes. "Most of them."

"Indeed." Liz grabbed the large basket full of spicy-smelling ornaments. "Two of our guests don't appear to enjoy anything that the Olde Mansion Inn has to offer."

"It does seem so," Sarah said softly.

When Liz reached the sitting room, she found that her most problematic guests were not present. Instead, Sadie sat in the middle of one of the sofas, telling the worst Christmas jokes Liz had ever heard.

"What do you get when you cross Father Christmas with a detective?" Sadie asked the guests who were perched on the furniture around her.

"I couldn't begin to guess," Mary Ann's cousin Arthur said, smiling.

"Santa Clues!"

The group groaned and laughed at the same time. Seeing their obvious good humor brightened Liz's mood immediately, and she didn't have to force the cheer into her voice as she explained about the decorations. "I thought we could start a Christmas tradition by trimming the tree in here."

"What a wonderful idea," Vivian said, popping up from where she sat on the edge of one of the cushy Victorian sofas. She peered into the basket of ornaments and took a deep sniff. "Those smell nearly as yummy as the cookies."

"But they're not nearly as tasty," Sadie warned as she bit the head off one of Naomi's gingerbread men. "Which reminds me, what's the best thing to put a Christmas cookie in?"

The group called out in unison, "What?"

"Your mouth!" Sadie said, breaking into uproarious laughter at her own joke.

Shaking her head at the punch line, Liz handed Sadie an applesauce-dough heart and then gave Vivian a sheep that wore a tiny red ribbon around its neck. Liz chose a pig for herself. They crossed to the fir tree that filled up an entire corner of the room.

Vivian studied the tree carefully before placing her ornament. "I love decorating the Christmas tree. It reminds me of my childhood."

"Me too," Mrs. Shelton said. She and her husband hung decorations as a team, with Mrs. Shelton seated in a nearby chair giving Mr. Shelton directions on where to place each ornament.

The elderly sisters showed no such teamwork and squabbled lightheartedly over who got to hang ornaments on what they perceived as the choicest branches. As the group decorated the tree, each person sampled Naomi's gorgeous cookies. All in all, it was exactly the sort of experience Liz had hoped for, even with Sadie's silly jokes.

After carrying in the trays, Mary Ann had stayed, but Sarah had excused herself and left the room to gather her things to go home for the evening. To Liz's surprise, Sarah leaned back through the doorway when the basket of ornaments was nearly empty. "Miss Eckardt?" she said. "There's someone to see you in the foyer, a Charlie Newman."

For a moment, Liz had no idea who that was, but then she remembered the storyteller. "Oh, right." She turned to her guests. "I'll be right back with a special guest."

"I'll keep things going here," Sadie promised.

Liz strode out to the foyer and found the young man gazing out the front windows. "Mr. Newman?"

The storyteller turned to face Liz. "Call me Charlie, please. I'm sorry. I know I'm a little late."

"No, your timing is perfect. We're finishing up some tree trimming. I know everyone will love hearing a story." *Especially after Sadie's jokes.*

"I'll do my best to please," Charlie said as he followed Liz back to the sitting room. The large basket of dough ornaments sat empty on the carved cherry coffee table, but the fir still looked a little bare. Liz wished she hadn't let the Christmas tree salesman talk her into such a large tree, even if it was beautifully shaped. She shook off the thought and smiled at the people now seated on the room's cushy Victorian sofas.

"Liz, you missed the joke," Sadie said. "What do you get if you deep-fry Santa?"

Liz wrinkled her nose and shook her head. "I'm afraid to ask."

"Crisp Kringle!" Sadie hooted.

Liz heard the storyteller chuckle at the joke, and she resisted the urge to groan along with the rest of the group. "As much as Sadie is a tough act to follow, I have a treat for all of you—a professional storyteller! Charlie has promised us a wonderful Christmas tale."

Vivian clapped her hands enthusiastically. "Perfect, just perfect. Will it have the Amish in it?"

Charlie nodded. "Yes, ma'am."

"Wonderful!" Vivian turned to look at Liz with wide eyes. "Do you think we could string popcorn while we listen? It's such a cozy old-fashioned activity and—" she glanced toward the tree—"I thought the tree might be even nicer with a garland."

Liz smiled back at her. "That's a lovely idea. I'll go put on some popcorn while Charlie begins the story."

As Liz headed for the door, Mary Ann met her and whispered, "I'll get needles and thread from Sew Welcome. And we have some red beads that would make great accents, like cranberries."

"Wonderful idea," Liz whispered back. "Please put the things on my tab."

Mary Ann nodded and the two separated.

In the kitchen, Liz retrieved the hot-air popper from a cupboard, feeling glad that she had it. The popcorn might taste a little like packing material, but it wouldn't be too greasy for stringing. As she poured in a big helping of popcorn kernels, the kitchen door opened and Liz turned to see Mary Ann carrying in a parcel wrapped in brown paper.

"Oh no," Liz said. "Not another one. Where did you find it?"

"In front of the shop door." Mary Ann carefully set down the package on one of the tall stools. Both women stared at the brown wrapping. Mary Ann had already torn back a corner to reveal the bright blue paper underneath.

With a shudder, Liz realized exactly what the package meant. For someone to leave it in front of Sew Welcome, the person must have come into the inn. If that person had used the front door, he or she would have had to walk right past the sitting room unnoticed, which seemed unlikely. Since the side door was unlocked, someone could have come in that way, walked through the utility room, and left the package by the shop's door.

But who was prowling through the house while we were trimming the tree?

8

Neither Liz nor Mary Ann could bring herself to touch the package as it lay on the stool, let alone carry it to the utility room and open it. It looked so harmless, but Liz remembered Jackson's concern that the person leaving the boxes could be upping his or her game.

"Can I help?" Sadie's voice boomed from the kitchen doorway as she burst in. "That storyteller is sweet, but not many laughs." She stopped when she spotted the parcel. "Not another one!"

"It was left for us," Mary Ann whispered. "Right outside the shop."

"This is one time I wouldn't have minded being left out," Sadie said. "What are we going to do with it?"

"Call the police?" Liz suggested.

"If it were up to me," Sadie said, "I'd wait until after the social. You don't want to upset the guests."

Liz had to agree. "I don't think they'd appreciate knowing the person leaving these terrible packages was right inside with them." Then she looked up at her friends as a horrifying idea struck her. "Do you think it's one of the guests? They all seem so nice. Well, except for Matt and that Brecken woman."

Sadie poked the package with her finger, making the box wobble slightly on the stool. "We've had people coming in and out all day, and we had a huge rush at closing time. With everyone so busy, I suppose we might have overlooked that thing. The person who left it wouldn't have to be a guest."

"True," Liz said, though she couldn't shake the suspicion that Matt was involved somehow. After all, he hadn't attended the guest social gathering, so he definitely could have been slinking around leaving nasty packages. If only she knew why he was in town, it would help. She was sure it wasn't lovesick longing on his part. So what was he after? Liz grabbed the big bowl of freshly popped corn. "We'll hold off until everyone leaves. Then I'm calling *someone* about this."

"That sounds wise," Mary Ann said as she poured more popcorn into the maker to busy herself. "I'll bring out this batch as soon as it's done." She looked at Sadie. "I completely forgot about getting the needles and thread and red beads from Sew Welcome. Can you get them for Liz?"

"I'm on it." Sadie turned on her heel and beat Liz through the door.

When Liz returned to the sitting room carrying the first batch of popcorn, she was surprised to see Portia sitting primly in one of the straight-backed chairs near the wall. As Liz set the bowl on the big coffee table, Sadie bustled in with the rest of the supplies, handing them out to anyone interested.

Liz took a needle and thread from Sadie and offered them to Portia but received a cold shake of the head. "I don't take part in hayseed crafts. Thank you anyway."

Resisting the urge to poke the annoying woman with the needle in her hand, Liz sat on the sofa beside Vivian instead and began threading popcorn.

Charlie, who had paused in his introduction as Liz and Sadie entered, launched back into his story, his voice as warm and rich as the crackling fire he stood beside. He told the small group about how the flu had swept through the small community in his tale, sending even some of the strongest farmers to bed to recuperate. He added that the farmers all recovered, but a little girl named Bea had a harder time. Then he slipped into a quiet voice as he moved deeper into the story, introducing the sick child's big sister, Annie.

"Annie desired nothing more than to give her little sister the gift she wanted most for Christag," he said. "Like most Amish girls, she'd been sewing since she was big enough to pick up a needle, but what materials could she use to make her sister a doll?"

He let the question hang in the air for a moment and then shook his head sadly. "The year had been a hard one, made no easier by the weeks of work the flu had stolen from the girls' father. Annie's mother's scrap box had been emptied, used for patching the family's clothes. There was no extra cloth for something frivolous like a doll."

Liz slipped popcorn and beads onto her needle absently, already caught up in the story of the little Amish girls. She barely noticed when Mary Ann snuck quietly into the room with another bowl of popcorn and took a seat next to Arthur.

"Sadly, Annie looked down at her sleeping sister. Little Bea's eyes fluttered in her sleep. Annie swept her gaze across the pegs that lined the room and held the girls' clothes, and the side table occupied by a vase of juniper branches. Under the vase was Annie's favorite thing in all the world—the linen mat with the beautiful blue edging that she had made to practice her stitches. Mutter had said the mat belonged to her, which is why it always rested on the small table."

Charlie paused to look around the room, and Liz stole a quick peek at her guests, happy to see them all entranced by Charlie's story. Even Portia sat forward in her chair, her normally haughty face softened by concern.

"Annie loved the mat, but she loved her little sister far more. She carefully cut the linen and the beautiful blue edging into pieces for little Bea's doll. By the flickering light of the candle, Annie stitched with her smallest, most precise stitches. This would be the perfect gift, and the joy of it would bring a smile back to little Bea's face."

Liz looked around the room again, expecting to find every eye on Charlie. To her surprise, she caught Portia glaring at her.

The unexpected hostility took Liz aback. *What did I ever do to her to warrant such a dirty look?* Portia quickly averted her gaze, and Liz wondered what kind of secrets the frosty woman might have. Why would she direct so much venom at a virtual stranger? And if Portia hated being at the inn so much, why in the world didn't she just leave? Liz would gladly refund her money. *What is keeping Portia Brecken in Pleasant Creek?*

Maybe she was being forced to stay in town by something or someone . . . Could her anger and resentment at being stuck in Pleasant Creek drive her to leave the disgusting boxes around town with the *Heartless* cards? Or were the packages the whole reason she'd come in the first place?

Somehow Liz couldn't quite picture the well-dressed woman shoving a dead mouse in a box for the bakery, but people had surprised her before. For that matter, any of the guests could be hiding hatred for the town, something terrible that would motivate them to leave the packages. The Sheltons, for instance, had married in Pleasant Creek, so they had a history with the town. But Mrs. Shelton didn't look well enough for such deceptions, and Mr. Shelton hardly seemed the type to abandon his poor wife to deliver rotting rodents about town. Still, Liz had learned the hard way that some people were very good at disguising their true natures.

That any of her guests were involved was hard to fathom at that moment, though, with each face reflecting total absorption in Charlie's story—well, each face other than Portia's, which was contorted in another evil glare directed at Liz.

Liz realized she'd missed some of Charlie's story during her musings and tuned back in, letting the storyteller engage her again.

". . . When Bea's tiny fingers tugged at the wrappings, Annie could hardly stand still. Finally, she reached over to give her sister a hand, pulling free the borrowed dishcloth to reveal the gift—a tiny doll with a sweet smile and beautiful blue dress." Charlie's voice turned light and sweet like a child's. "'She is the most beautiful doll in the world!' Bea exclaimed."

"And the kid got better, and everyone lived happily ever after." Matt's painfully familiar voice dripped with scorn.

"I see you know the story." Charlie smiled amiably at Matt, who had appeared in the doorway with a beautifully wrapped present under his arm.

"Only because it's how all those sticky-sweet Christmas stories end. Real life doesn't work that way."

"Which is why I prefer stories," Charlie said agreeably. "As you said, life is often unkind, especially to those who deserve unkindness least. But what kind of Christag story would it be if the little girl died?"

"A realistic one. Some of us live in the real world. We don't need fairy tales."

"Charlie, I'm sorry your wonderful story was interrupted," Liz said. "Thank you so much for sharing it with us." She turned to Matt, shooting daggers at him with her eyes. "Did you want something?"

He held up the gift he'd tried to give her when he'd arrived and carried it over to the tree. "I wanted to be the first to put a present under your Christmas tree." The present's shiny wrapping contrasted sharply with the tree, half decorated in homemade trimmings. "A little something to remind you of Boston and all the fantastic things you can find there."

Liz fought the urge to pick up the box and fling it at him. She didn't want to upset her guests, who wouldn't understand her anger toward this slick, charismatic man. Still, she watched him closely, with the same wary attention she'd give a snake in the yard. "You missed the beginning of the story," she said. "I wonder what kept you."

"I was chatting with my grandfather." Matt gave her his most charming smile. "Family is so important, and you know how close mine is. He sends his love."

The cheery twins beamed at him for that comment. "It's nice to see a young man who appreciates the value of family," Gina Fritz said, patting her sister's hand.

Matt turned his smile toward her. "A close family shares its joys and burdens. I can see you two lovely ladies are the sort that does exactly that."

Lois Granger nodded so enthusiastically that the festive plaid headband she'd donned for the evening slipped forward. "Definitely."

"It can be hard when you're all alone," Vivian added, turning mournful eyes toward Matt.

"No one should be by themselves at Christmas," he said sincerely, coming over to squeeze in between Liz and Vivian on the sofa. "We can all be part of one another's family this year."

Liz resisted the impulse to make gagging sounds at Matt's obvious effort to cozy up to her guests. Surely they would soon see how patently fake he was acting . . . but no one seemed to have figured it out yet. One by one, each of the guests was swept up in his false warmth. He charmed them so completely they seemed to forget about the boorish way he had ruined Charlie's story. Even Charlie smiled and nodded as Matt continued to gush about family.

In desperation, Liz looked toward Mary Ann and Sadie. They both eyed Matt skeptically, though Sadie's glares were more pointed. At least Liz could count on her friends to see Matt for the snake he was.

Then to Liz's surprise, she noticed one other person who didn't seem charmed by Matt's act at all. Portia sat painfully straight in her chair and watched Matt with the same stark condemnation that Liz suspected her own face showed. Portia had been Matt's champion when he first arrived, but he'd clearly fallen out of her favor. Of course, considering the snooty woman's attitude in general, she could simply disapprove of him consorting with the rest of the guests instead of her.

"Ms. Eckardt?" Charlie's voice snapped Liz's attention away from Portia. "I need to be on my way." Liz rose and accompanied the young man out of the room into the foyer. He turned to look at her shyly. "I'll be back tomorrow night with a new story, if you'll have me."

"Certainly," she agreed readily. "I just realized we never worked out payment. Should I write you a check now? I didn't even ask about your rates."

Charlie smiled warmly and quoted a figure that made Liz blink. The man barely wanted to be paid at all. Liz loved a bargain as much as the next person, but she didn't want to cheat the man.

"That doesn't seem like nearly enough," she said.

"It's plenty. Telling my stories is its own reward. I learn so much about the people I meet this way. I'll bring an invoice on the last night, and you can pay me then."

Liz decided she'd add a big tip when that time came. She left Charlie to put on his coat and returned to her guests. "Charlie will be back tomorrow with another story."

Everyone clapped and thanked her for having the young storyteller. To Liz's surprise, Matt joined in the enthusiasm before jumping up and rushing out of the room. She followed him and found he'd caught Charlie at the front door. Matt was shaking the younger man's hand.

"I hope you'll come for my next story," Charlie said. "I'll try to make the ending more of a surprise."

"And I'll try to be less of a critic." Matt's tone was almost gracious.

Liz rolled her eyes as she walked by Matt to let Charlie out. She locked the door behind him and peered out the window at the night. The arrival of one of the loathsome parcels right inside her home had left Liz jumpy, even if she did suspect more and more that the packages were part of some strange plan of Matt's. She kept her back to her ex until she heard him retreat to the sitting room.

Liz followed at a safe distance and entered the room to find the guests draping their garlands of popcorn and red beads on the tree.

"This has been a lovely evening, but I'm ready to head up to my room for some reading," Vivian announced. "I hope we can string more popcorn tomorrow night." She leaned closer to Liz and whispered, "The tree is still a little bare."

"A little," Liz agreed as the woman passed her and headed out the door. She looked at the tree sadly and wondered what else she could put on it.

"I think it's going to be lovely," Gina said as she patted Liz's arm. "Though we won't be able to string popcorn tomorrow night. We're going to the candlelight tour of homes that we saw in the pamphlet you left in our room."

"It sounds lovely," Lois said.

"But we'll certainly be at the next storytelling night," Gina assured her. "My sister and I are having a wonderful stay so far."

"We are," Lois said enthusiastically. "And we think your young man is charming."

Gina gave Liz a sly wink. "Very charming. Don't let that one get away."

Before Liz could refute their idea that Matt was *her* young man, the two sisters scurried from the room, chatting about Christmas ornaments.

"I think your young man is charming too," Matt said, speaking so close to Liz's ear that the tickle of his breath made her jump.

"You're not mine," she said through clenched teeth.

"For now." He strolled from the room, whistling *Winter Wonderland*. It made Liz want to throw something at him.

Liz noticed that Portia left soon after, though the woman clearly felt no urge to bid Liz good night first.

After Mary Ann gave Arthur a good night hug, she turned to Liz and pointed. "Kitchen," she mouthed silently.

Liz nodded.

Mr. Shelton spoke from one of the sofas, where he sat holding hands with his wife. "We're going to stay and enjoy the fire for a while, if that's all right, Liz. This is such a beautiful room."

"Of course." Liz smiled at the couple before she and Sadie headed to the kitchen to face the package still perched on the stool. She found Mary Ann putting the popcorn bowls in the sink and giving the package anxious glances.

"You two don't have to stay," Liz said. "I'm going to call Jackson and hand this awful thing over to him. But first, I'm taking it to the utility room."

The mention of Jackson seemed to brighten Mary Ann's and Sadie's faces. Liz suspected she was going to be in for some more teasing from her friends about the handsome mayor, so she hurried out of the room with the package gingerly held away from her body.

When she got back to the kitchen, her friends grinned at each other as Liz made the call. Jackson answered on the first ring and promised to be right over.

While Liz spoke to him, Sadie and Mary Ann busied themselves filling the sink to wash the popcorn bowls and cookie trays. But it was clear to Liz that they were both listening attentively to her end of the conversation, so she took care to sound strictly professional. "Come around to the utility room door, please," she said at the end of the call. "I've locked up the front entrance for the night."

When she turned her attention back to her friends, Sadie's eyebrows climbed nearly to the bottom of her white bangs. "It's interesting that you called Jackson instead of the police. You see this as a job for the mayor?"

"He seems the most interested." Liz shoved her phone into her pocket. "I think the police are still writing it off as a teen prank.

When Jackson and I went out to talk to Miriam, we found out the Amish are getting packages too."

"Oh?" Sadie smiled slyly. "You and Jackson are teaming up to investigate this? That's an excellent idea. I hope you're working closely together."

Liz frowned, covering her embarrassment by plunging her hands into the sink and washing the dishes. "This is serious. Naomi was very upset to have a dead mouse brought into her bakery. And you both said yourselves that having one of these dumped inside the inn is bad for business."

Mary Ann retrieved a towel to dry a bowl as Liz finished rinsing it. "We do take the packages seriously. Sadie enjoys teasing you, obviously, but you can't totally blame her. You and Jackson make a cute couple. And we've known him all his life, so we like seeing him interested in someone we like as much as you."

"Jackson's interest right now is in discovering who is leaving these repulsive packages. I'm simply helping."

"That's one thing we like about you," Mary Ann said. "You're *so* helpful."

"Besides," Sadie added, "be honest. You've noticed how good-looking he is."

Liz had no intention of being honest about that. "I assure you, I've learned my lesson about handsome men." She rubbed a soapy cloth over the second bowl with more vigor than was necessary. "Matt is making me crazy. I don't know why he's here, but I wonder if it might be connected with these packages."

"You really think Matt is leaving them?" Mary Ann asked.

Sadie crossed her arms over her chest. "We should have let Beans bite him."

"I don't know anything for sure, but he's not staying at my inn because he's pining away for me, no matter what he says."

"You don't think a man could pine away for you?" Mary Ann

asked mildly, wiping at the bowl Liz handed her. "I disagree."

"In theory, maybe. In Matt's case, no." Liz rinsed off the last cookie tray. "He doesn't do anything that doesn't benefit him. All of Matt's love is for Matt."

"You know him better than we do," Mary Ann said.

"We'll keep an eye on him," Sadie offered. "After all, if Beans hates him, he's got to be bad news."

When the dishes were done, Liz shooed her friends along home for the night, assuring them that she could finish the tidying up while she waited for Jackson.

"We'll go," Sadie said. "But only so you have some alone time with Jackson. You need to call me and let me know what was in the package. I won't sleep if I don't hear from you."

"I'll call," Liz promised. She turned to Mary Ann. "Should I call you too?"

Mary Ann wrapped her arms around herself. "No, thank you. Tomorrow is soon enough. I hate the idea of getting one of those awful things in the first place. I don't need the nightmares from picturing what's inside."

"Whatever is in there, I'm sure it's not personal," Liz said. "No one could think you or Sadie is heartless. Not if they know you at all."

Mary Ann gave her a grateful smile and left with Sadie.

Liz finished tidying the kitchen, wondering when Jackson would arrive. She knew it hadn't been long since she made the call, but she was still getting antsy. Her thoughts kept wandering to the package. It didn't smell as far as she could tell, but she suspected that would change once it was unwrapped. "Nothing dead," she whispered with a shudder. "Just . . . please, nothing dead."

The crash of a garbage can being overturned outside jerked her from her thoughts and drew her quickly through the utility room to the side door. She flung the door open. An exterior light brightened the side patio, but beyond that, shadows deepened. In the murky darkness, Liz could just make out two tall male figures scuffling in the night.

Swallowing her panic, Liz yelled, "Stop! I've called the police!"

9

Neither of the men responded to Liz as they continued to grapple. One figure had launched himself at the other and now they struggled, clinging to each other and trying to land punches at the same time. Liz fumbled for the switch to the back floodlights. Finally, her hand hit the lever, and the bright light brought the two combatants into sharp focus. Jackson had Matt by the collar of his jacket, while her ex tried to get free.

"Matthew Richard Sheridan!" she hollered. "What are you doing?"

"Me?" Matt yelped, still struggling against Jackson's grip. "He attacked me!"

Jackson gave Matt one last shake before releasing him. "I saw someone skulking around in the dark. I called out, and he ran. I stopped him so we could have a chat."

"You *assaulted* me." Matt tugged at his jacket, smoothing wrinkles and picking bits of debris from his hair. "And, by the way, it's cold out here. Can we continue this indoors?"

Liz stepped aside. "I suppose. But don't think you're getting out of answering my questions."

Matt stormed past her into the utility room with Jackson right behind him. "You know, it's not going to impress people when I tell them I got mugged at your inn."

Jackson took a step closer to Matt, using his scant inch of extra height and much broader shoulders to loom menacingly. "I dealt with an intruder, which you certainly appeared to be. Now tell us what had you out lurking in the dark before the police arrive."

"The police!" Matt pushed his face toward Jackson and glared. "I'm a guest of this inn."

"Only because you forced your way in," Liz said. "But I haven't actually called the police. Yet."

"Go ahead and call the cops. I'm still a guest here," Matt said. "What do you think the police will do when they find out this guy is mugging the inn's guests?"

"I suppose they'll ask, 'Why did you need to restrain him, Mr. Mayor?'" Jackson answered.

Matt turned a shocked expression toward Liz. "This guy is the mayor?"

Liz simply nodded.

Matt groaned. "Fine. I don't owe you an explanation, but because I'm a good citizen, I'll tell you anyway."

"Thank you so much," Liz said.

"I saw how jumpy you were acting in the sitting room tonight, so I eavesdropped a little on you and those two old hens in the kitchen after everyone else left. I heard about the package left inside the inn, and I thought I'd investigate outside to see if there was any sign of someone getting in through a window."

"And why would you do that?"

Matt shrugged. "I figured if I could find out who left you that package, you'd stop thinking it was me and give me a chance. I do want you to come back to Boston with me for Christmas. I'm being completely sincere about that."

Sincere wasn't a word that Liz ever connected with Matt. In fact, Liz doubted every other word out of his mouth most of the time. Even when they had been together, he'd rarely given her a straight answer that didn't have some kind of spin on it. She glanced at Jackson and could tell by his expression that he didn't believe Matt any more than she did.

"And did you find anything?" Liz asked her ex.

Matt shook his head. "I might have, if this guy hadn't attacked me." He looked from Liz to Jackson, scowling at both.

Liz realized she wasn't going to get anything useful out of him. "Fine. You wanted to be a big help. Thanks."

Matt looked at her in surprise and blinked. "That's it?" He turned to glare again at Jackson. "No apology for attacking me?"

"No," Jackson said.

Matt's eyes narrowed. "This isn't over."

"We can still call the police," Jackson said. "You can tell your whole 'creeping around outside to help Liz' story again. They love a good joke."

Matt didn't respond to that; he merely glowered for another moment. Then he stormed out of the utility room.

Liz watched him leave with a mixture of frustration and hopelessness. As much as she wanted to throw him out, Matt knew a lot of people. And some of them even actually liked him. Could he ruin her business? She wasn't sure.

"Try not to worry," Jackson said. "He's clearly here for a specific purpose, and I don't think it involves ruining you."

Liz looked at Jackson sharply, shocked by his apparent mind reading.

He smiled. "I heard his remark about telling people he got mugged at your inn. That's publicity no one would want, but I don't think he'd go through with it. He obviously wants you to do something, and I don't think he's going to alienate you that much. It would be counterproductive. But who is he?"

"That is my ex-boyfriend, Matt Sheridan. He showed up here from Boston out of the blue. I know he wants something from me, but I don't really know what—yet. I know he doesn't care about being with me, and I've made it clear I don't want to be with him." She sighed. "Whatever his motivation, is it enough to make him leave these disgusting things around town?" She gave the package on the table a poke.

"Good question. I wish I had an answer for you. But exes have a way of knowing which buttons to push. I'd try not to worry about it." Jackson picked up the package and turned it over in his hands. "Right now, there's only one question we can answer: What is in this box?" He set the parcel back on the table and pulled out his mobile phone. "Would you film me opening it?"

Liz took the phone and started recording. Jackson turned the box so Liz could capture the intact package from every angle. Then he carefully peeled off the brown paper, and Liz moved in for a close-up of the all-too-familiar fancy layer underneath. Jackson turned back the edge of the ornate wrapping, and Liz reached out to feel the paper.

"Do all the packages have the same blue paper?" she asked. "This certainly looks like the paper that was on the one left outside here and the one I saw at the bakery."

"I haven't seen all of them," Jackson said. "But of the ones I've seen, yeah, I think the paper has been consistent."

"It's unusual though, don't you think?"

"Unusual how?"

"It's thick. Almost too thick for holiday wrap because it's rather stiff for folding. It's nearly as thick as the brown paper on the outside of the packages, and the design is fairly abstract. It looks vaguely Christmassy because of the foil snowflakes. But it's blue, not red or green, and there's no Santa or holly or any of the usual holiday motifs."

Jackson felt the paper and nodded. "Good point. And this silver accent is slightly raised." He smiled at Liz. "I think we ought to track down this paper." He carefully removed the rest of the shiny layer and opened the box.

The smell of old hay and mold filled the room, and Liz wrinkled her nose. "Same smell as mine. Without the dead-mouse kicker that Naomi's box had." She peeked into the box and saw the expected *Heartless* card lying on the pile of hay with a few stray bits of ragged cloth.

"Do you have something we can use to cover the table?" Jackson asked. "I think I see something glinting in all this hay, but I don't want to stick my hand in. I'd rather dump out the box."

Liz retrieved a trash bag and laid it over the table. Jackson carefully shook out the contents of the box. The hay and old rags fell with barely any sound, but something else tumbled out of the container and thunked against the table. Liz leaned closer to see.

"Glass," Jackson said quietly. "That's new." He pulled an ink pen from his shirt pocket and used it to turn over the thick shard. Along one edge, the glass was discolored with dark brown stains.

"Do you think that's blood?" Liz whispered.

"I think it's time to call in the police for this one. If that is blood, they're going to need to be involved so we can find out what it's from."

"What . . . or who?"

"That's what I'm worried about." Jackson took his phone back from Liz and called the police. Liz stared at the shard of glass, mesmerized by the dark stains.

"Could any of your guests have seen whoever dropped this off at Sew Welcome?" Jackson asked after ending his call, startling Liz out of her preoccupied stare.

"Mary Ann and Sadie definitely didn't see anyone suspicious. And I didn't either. If it was dropped off at the end of the business day or during the social time—which seems likely—most of the guests were in the sitting room with us. We would have noticed someone coming in the front door, but someone could have come in through this side door and then left the package at Sew Welcome with none of us seeing. But they'd have to be familiar with the layout of the inn to even know to use the side door in the first place."

"You said most of your guests were in the sitting room? But not all?"

Liz shook her head. "Two of the guests didn't join us until around the time the storytelling started."

Jackson gave her a mirthless smile. "Let me guess—one of the two was Matt Sheridan."

Liz nodded. "And the other was Portia Brecken. She hasn't been an overly pleasant guest either and, honestly, she's just strange. She hates me, hates the inn, hates Pleasant Creek, yet won't leave. I found her up on the third floor one day, even though her room is on the second floor." Liz gave herself a mental shake. "Though really, lots of guests explore the inn. It's simple curiosity. And the third floor is certainly not off-limits to any guest here. It was only odd because she has made it clear that she doesn't like the inn. Her behavior is hard to explain."

"It's all right," Jackson said. "You're not accusing her of anything. Right now, it's wise to notice aberrations."

They went into the kitchen, and Liz fixed a pot of decaf coffee while they waited for the police to arrive. She made a quick call to Sadie to tell her what the box contained, promising a more detailed report in the morning. It wasn't long before she heard a knock at the side door, and she and Jackson went to the utility room to answer it.

Liz was surprised to see Stan Houghton, the police chief, standing there with another officer.

At her look of astonishment, the chief said, "If the mayor considers this important, so do I. Plus, I don't like the way these packages are multiplying."

"Is this not the only new package?" Jackson asked.

Chief Houghton shook his head. "Tom Yoder got one over at the funeral home this morning. It had the head of an old teddy bear in it. If that was a joke, Tom wasn't amused."

"I'd imagine not," Liz said, suddenly glad she had a warm mug of coffee to ward off the chill.

Liz offered cups to the police chief and the officer who accompanied him, but the chief declined for both of them. "He'll just take some pictures and gather up the evidence. Then we'll be on our way."

"Decapitated teddy bears, shards of glass with what looks like blood, dead animals," Jackson said. "If there's a message here, it's vague."

The chief pinched the business card up from the collection of debris. "And this doesn't exactly make anything clearer. Is it an accusation or a confession?"

"It's almost scarier this way," Liz said. "It feels threatening, but there's no clue as to what kind of threat it is." She pulled her gaze from the pile of debris to lock eyes with the police chief. "You don't still think this is a kid's prank, do you?"

He rubbed a hand across his ample stomach and rocked on his toes. "I don't know what to think."

"I do," Jackson said. "I think it's time to put a stop to it."

"How do you suggest we do that, Mr. Mayor?" Chief Houghton asked. "It's Christmas. Half my force is out of the office, and the ones I have left wish they were. I can't exactly stake out every store that hasn't gotten a package on the off chance they're going to get one."

"We have to figure out something."

The chief nodded. "I'm open to suggestions—as soon as you have one to offer."

With nothing more to say and the package contents bagged as evidence, the chief and the officer prepared to leave.

"Excuse me," Liz said. "Could I have a small sample of that wrapping paper? I want to try to track down where it came from."

The chief frowned and rubbed his hand over his chin. "Ordinarily, I'd tell you to let us handle it, but since I'm shorthanded, I'll make an exception." He nodded to the officer, who carefully clipped off a piece of the paper and handed it to Liz. "But you be careful. If you turn up anything, call my office. Don't take any risks."

Liz held up her hands in mock surrender. "No worries. I don't have any interest in coming face to face with this person."

"Good." The chief shooed the officer out the door and followed in his wake.

Jackson hung back. "Do you want me to help you to check out possible sources for the wrapping paper?"

Liz smiled at him. "Thanks, but I can handle it. Shopping for wrapping paper isn't exactly a dangerous activity."

Jackson retuned her smile. "I don't know. It is Christmas. You don't want to get between a shopper and the last roll of their favorite gift wrap."

"I'll try to stay safe."

Jackson's expression turned serious once again. "You do that."

After he left, Liz took her nightly walk around the main floor of the inn, checking that all the doors and windows were locked up tight. The Sheltons had left the sitting room, and Liz saw the fire was nearly out in the fireplace. As she bent to deal with the embers, she heard a noise. She stood and crept toward the doorway, where she realized it was two people arguing somewhere upstairs.

As quietly as possible, she followed the sound out through the dark foyer, creeping closer to the staircase. Liz was fairly certain one voice was male and one female, but she couldn't make out any of the words or hear clearly enough to recognize either voice. That both parties were furious was clear, though. Liz inched closer still.

Who's arguing at this time of night, and why?

10

Liz was determined to find out who was arguing upstairs. Unfortunately, the foyer was very dark and Beans must have decided his favorite rug wasn't as comfortable as the center of the rotunda. She tripped over the dog, and Beans woke with a yelp. Liz flew over his wide back and landed hard on the floor.

She scrambled to her feet as quickly as she could, quite a feat considering Beans seemed determined to get in the way as much as possible. By the time she limped around the dog and over to the base of the steps, the voices were silent. Liz peered up the dark stairs, but she saw no sign of anyone. Could it have been Matt's voice? But who would he argue with besides her?

After another night of spotty sleep, Liz shuffled to the kitchen to start her work for the day, her head feeling stuffed with wool. She'd chosen a cheerful Christmas sweater that wasn't too whimsical in the hopes of jollying herself into more of the yuletide spirit. So far, it hadn't worked.

She spotted Beans standing next to the kitchen door. He watched patiently as she got the coffee brewing, but then he whined.

"I know," she said. "Nature calls. Let me get your leash, because we are not having a repetition of our wild chase through the yard. That was embarrassing for both of us."

Beans responded with a *whuff* and trailed her into the utility room. Liz grabbed the leash and her coat from a rack, and led him out. The sun had not yet risen, though the sky was lightening with the promise of the dawn. Dampness sharpened the morning chill, and Liz looked up at the dark sky, wondering idly if it might snow. With Steve not coming home, she no longer cared much about a white Christmas, but she thought the guests might enjoy seeing some falling flakes.

When Beans finally finished sniffing all the shrubbery and doing his other outdoor business, the sky was noticeably lighter, and pink colored the horizon. Liz hustled the dog back toward the side door. "I need to get going on breakfast," she scolded him as he smelled a bare bush for the third time. "I have actual guests now and don't want to be late." She finally resorted to bending over and hauling the dog up the last few steps. "I'm going to need a chiropractor for Christmas at this rate," she grumbled as she huffed and puffed.

Once they were in the utility room, Beans seemed to find his legs again. He walked calmly into the kitchen and lapped at his water bowl. "Sometimes I wish you were a cat," Liz said on her way to the sink to wash up.

She'd planned a welcoming breakfast of French toast made with some tasty bread from Naomi's bakery. As she cut thick slices, she looked up at the clock and suddenly became worried. *Where is Sarah?* The girl knew Liz was already shorthanded with the other part-time helper, Kiera, gone to Indianapolis to spend Christmas with her mom's family. It wasn't like the conscientious young woman to be late.

Though she worked as quickly as she could, every minute heightened Liz's concern for Sarah. She was beating eggs into a froth when Mary Ann poked her head into the kitchen. "I was hoping to grab a cup of coffee and hear about last night with as few gory details as possible."

"Help yourself. Have you seen Sarah?"

Mary Ann's pleasant face creased in a frown. "She's not in yet?"

"No, and frankly, I'm worried."

Mary Ann carried her coffee over and looked at Liz's breakfast fixings. "Can I help?"

Liz gave her a grateful smile. "If you don't mind cutting up fruit. I need to get the bacon ready for the broiler. I'm hoping Sarah comes soon, though. I wanted to get out of here right after breakfast to check out some possible sources of the wrapping paper in those mystery packages." Liz went on to describe the events Mary Ann had missed the night before.

Mary Ann sighed. "I know you're helping Jackson, but I hate to see those horrible packages pull anyone's attention off Christmas."

"I promise not to lose my perspective." Liz gestured at her sweater with one hand before she began folding bacon into loose loops and laying them on a broiler pan. "Didn't you see my Christmas spirit?"

Mary Ann smiled at the sweater. "It's nice, but Sadie's has you beat."

"I'm sure. My sweater is supposed to be cheering me up, but I'm jumpy. I'll feel better when we know what's going on. With two of those packages showing up here, they're already intruding on us. This isn't something I can ignore, so I might as well investigate."

Working together, the women soon had breakfast ready. As they carried the dishes of fluffy French toast, bacon and fresh fruit out to the dining room, they were met with gasps of admiration from the guests—well, most of the guests.

"I couldn't possibly eat anything this rich," Portia said, looking at one of the platters in horror. "There must be over a thousand calories on that plate."

"What can I get you instead?" Liz asked, forcing a pleasant tone into her voice. She must not have been overly successful hiding her attitude because Mary Ann gave her an amused glance before slipping off to Sew Welcome.

"The fruit will be fine, I suppose," Portia said wearily. "I don't suppose that you have any Greek yogurt to go with it."

"I do. I'll get you some right away."

"Personally, I can't imagine passing up anything this scrumptious," Vivian said from her place beside Portia at the long table. "This is amazing."

Liz noticed that Vivian had a folded newspaper beside her plate. She looked around the table and saw most of the guests had newspapers as well. Surely she wasn't running so late that everyone had had time to go out and buy a paper.

Portia's nasal voice pulled Liz's attention back to her. "I'm sure the food is more than adequate. If one doesn't care about one's waistline."

Vivian chuckled at Portia's snooty attitude and patted her stomach. "At least mine is happy." She turned her attention away and opened the paper to read while she ate her breakfast; two others quickly followed her example.

As Liz headed to the kitchen for the yogurt, she thought about why she didn't have the local paper delivered to the inn. She preferred her guests socialize over breakfast, but with Portia at the table and Matt probably on his way, maybe they were better off reading.

Liz stepped into the kitchen just as the side door was flung open, banging loudly against the utility room wall.

Sarah practically ran into the kitchen from the short hallway, her face splotchy and her eyes red. Her normally spotless dress was dirty along the hem, and her hair was slightly disarrayed. She caught sight of Liz and tried to adopt her usual quiet demeanor. "I'm sorry I'm late," the girl managed to say before her voice grew hoarse.

"Sarah, what's wrong? Did something happen at home? Is someone sick?" Liz gently led the girl to a stool to sit.

"No, the trouble wasn't at home." Sarah hiccupped as she fought back fresh tears. She blinked rapidly, turning damp green eyes toward Liz. "Mrs. Henderson is in the hospital."

"Mrs. Henderson?" Liz echoed. The name didn't sound familiar as she mentally ran through all of the Amish families she knew.

Sarah nodded. "She owns Mama's Home Cooking. Isaac and I deliver eggs to her restaurant several times a week. Actually, only once a week in the winter. The hens don't lay as well, and many won't lay at all this time of year."

Liz listened in surprise as the girl rambled. Sarah normally spoke little and had an immaculate appearance; she must be in shock from whatever had happened. "And you delivered eggs today?"

"We tried." Fresh tears filled Sarah's eyes, and Liz waited patiently for the girl to get herself under control again. "We always take them to the rear entrance, but when we arrived, the back door hung open. Mrs. Henderson was lying in the doorway." Again Sarah hesitated before whispering, "There was blood."

"Oh Sarah!" Liz hugged the young woman impulsively, but Sarah felt stiff in her arms. "What did you do?"

"I ran across the street to the grocery because they are always in early also. They called an ambulance. And the police came." At that, Sarah looked stricken again. "I am afraid. I know I should not be. We must trust Gött in all things, but I am afraid."

"Afraid?" Liz repeated. "Of the person who hurt Mrs. Henderson?"

Sarah shook her head. "Of the police. They asked so many questions about why we were there and what we saw. We did not see much, only Mrs. Henderson and the package."

"Package?"

"Like the one you got. Like the ones the community is finding in our buggies when we stop in town."

"The police can't possibly think you or Isaac had anything to do with the packages or with Mrs. Henderson's injury," Liz said. "Do you know if she's going to be all right?"

Sarah stared at her wide-eyed again. "Gött forgive me, I have had my eyes only on myself. I have hardly even prayed for Mrs. Henderson. I was so worried about Isaac, after his trouble with the police."

The past experience of her husband's false accusation had understandably left a painful impression on the young woman. "Sarah, Isaac was completely cleared and no one thinks ill of him now," Liz insisted. "I'm sure the police were only doing their job."

Sarah hiccupped and nodded. "I am certain you are right. All of this worry—it is not our way." She wiped at her eyes with a tissue Liz handed her and took a deep breath. "If they truly suspected Isaac, they would not have let us go after they asked their questions."

"Exactly," Liz said. "I'll call Jackson right after breakfast to be sure, if you wish. He has been very involved in investigating these packages, so he'll know if the police have any suspects."

Sarah offered a slightly watery smile. "*Dänka.* That would make me feel better. I should have faith." She cast her gaze around the room. "Now I am here. How can I help?"

"I've already served everyone . . . oh no." Liz remembered Portia's request for yogurt. The difficult guest was hardly likely to be happy with the wait. She spun, snatched a yogurt from the fridge, and practically ran it out to the dining room.

"I'm sorry for the delay," Liz said as she gave Portia the yogurt and a spoon.

The slender woman looked at the carton. "In that amount of time, I thought perhaps you had a cow in the kitchen and were making the yogurt from scratch. Imagine my disappointment."

"I hate to disrupt your view of country life, but I don't know how to make yogurt."

"How surprising. I thought you'd learn that sort of thing out here on the farm."

"This isn't a farm," Liz said with a tight smile.

"Of course not."

Liz fought her urge to yell at the tiresome woman by collecting empty dishes from guests who would not quite meet her eyes. For a moment, Liz wondered if their breakfast hadn't tasted as delicious as she'd hoped. Had she left out some vital ingredient in the French toast? She looked over at Gina and Lois, and saw they were sharing one of the newspapers. *Is the problem with the newspapers?*

"Excuse me, Miss Eckardt?" Mrs. Shelton said hesitantly. "Is it true that some sort of violent criminal is leaving dead animals at local businesses as a threat?"

Liz looked at her in horror. "Where did you hear such a thing?"

"In the *Pleasant Creek News & Views,*" Portia said, her mouth turned up in a cold smirk. "One of your local ace reporters, Rob Carver, has a front-page story this morning."

Liz looked around the room at the anxious faces.

"We thought you must know about the article," Mr. Shelton said. "The newspaper was right outside our room this morning, and the story quotes you directly."

"Mine was right outside my door too," Vivian said. Everyone else at the table echoed the statement. Someone had left a newspaper outside the door of each of the inn's guest rooms.

That's when Liz noticed Matt standing in the doorway, leaning nonchalantly against the frame with one ankle crossed over the other. His smile was distinctly gloating, and suddenly Liz felt quite sure she knew where the newspapers had come from.

"May I see the story?" she asked as calmly as possible.

Gina stood and handed Liz the newspaper she had been reading with her sister. Sure enough, the article made the packages sound as frightening and ghoulish as possible. Her own quote was brief, but the text around it led the reader to believe she was uncooperative because she feared for her life.

As Liz read, she thought of how much worse the next story would be after Rob got wind of what had happened that morning at Mrs. Henderson's restaurant. At this rate, she wasn't going to need Matt's bad review to ruin business.

"This reporter is making this sound much worse than it is," Liz said firmly. "The packages are annoying, but they aren't overtly threatening. None of the business owners are in fear of their lives."

"We were thinking of buying tickets to the candlelight house tour for this evening," Lois said. "Is it going to be safe for us to be out at night?"

"We wondered if we should stay in," her sister added. "And maybe stick to daytime events."

"I am sure the tour will be perfectly safe. It's conducted in groups and, honestly, Pleasant Creek is a very nice town."

"It doesn't seem all that nice to me," Portia said. "I don't remember anyone ever leaving dead animals on my stoop in Boston."

"It was only one little mouse!" Sadie's voice boomed from the doorway, and Liz winced. Sadie must have decided to check in on breakfast. It wouldn't be the first time the scent of bacon had lured her over from the shop. Still, Liz regretted her friend's timing and volume, and she cringed as Sadie continued. "Most of the boxes only had old hay and rags. Okay, there was that *one* with the bone, and the bloody glass that Liz found in the one last night . . ."

Liz gave Sadie a desperate look. *Stop helping.*

"There was another one last night?" Portia demanded. "I suppose I should be grateful we only found newspapers outside our doors today."

"Now, now," Mr. Shelton said. "The newspaper made it clear that these things are only found outside. I'm certain no one is coming into the inn."

"I wouldn't be so sure about that."

11

Liz glared at her ex and hissed through gritted teeth, "Matthew!"

"It just seems to me that they have a right to know about last night," Matt said with a gloating grin. "Especially since that package turned up inside this very inn, right next to the fabric shop."

"Inside!" Portia stood and tossed her napkin on the table. "I'll have to think carefully about whether I want to continue my stay here. It doesn't sound safe."

"I don't know," Vivian said cheerfully. "I appreciate a little excitement and mystery, and I certainly don't intend to let something silly keep me from enjoying this beautiful place." She smiled at Portia. "You said you live in the city? And you're afraid of a little dead mouse?"

"Not afraid. Disgusted."

Vivian shrugged. "Well, I for one intend to have a delightful time on the candlelight tour. The homes in the brochure were gorgeous."

The twin sisters leaned their heads together and talked quietly, as did the Sheltons.

After a moment, Mrs. Shelton said, "We weren't planning to go on the tour, but I certainly don't intend to cut our stay short." She smiled at Liz. "You've given us a lovely visit so far."

Liz thanked her guests as they each added their intention to ignore the newspaper story and focus on having a good Christmas.

Finally Portia tossed her head. "I suppose I'll stay. As long as nothing else happens."

Liz watched Portia stalk out of the room and hoped the woman *would* change her mind about staying.

As they cleaned up after breakfast, Sarah didn't mention Liz's promise to call Jackson, but Liz could feel the apprehension in every glance the young woman gave her. If anything, Sarah was even more diligent than usual, and the kitchen was soon back to its usual condition—radiantly tidy.

"I'll go take care of the dining room," Sarah said, though she lingered in the doorway a moment, something she never did.

"I'll call Jackson now," Liz promised her. "And I'll come find you the second I know anything."

Sarah bobbed her head and slipped through the door.

Jackson answered the phone on the first ring. "Hi, Liz."

"Have you heard about Mrs. Henderson from Mama's Home Cooking?" Liz asked.

"I have. In fact, I just got off the phone with the hospital. Her head got knocked pretty hard, but she's going to be fine."

Liz let out a breath she hadn't realized she was holding. "That's good. Sarah will be relieved. Did Mrs. Henderson get a look at whoever attacked her?"

"I don't know. She was unconscious when Isaac and Sarah found her, and she didn't wake up until a short while ago. I'm not sure if the chief has sent anyone to talk to her yet."

Liz sat down on one of the tall kitchen stools. "Sarah was very upset. I think she was worried that since Isaac found Mrs. Henderson, the police would have reason to believe he was involved. It would be helpful if I could allay that fear completely."

"You can. Tell her the police don't suspect Isaac at all. In fact, I expect Mrs. Henderson has a lot to be grateful for; she could have stayed out in the cold for another couple hours before anyone found her. She could have died from exposure."

"Sarah will be relieved to hear that." Liz began idly straightening a row of cookbooks on a shelf.

"Unfortunately, the police don't have any suspects at all. Though I might. I personally find it very suspicious that Matt was skulking around outside in the dark last night."

"Normally, I would too," Liz said. "But a physical attack on a woman just isn't Matt's style."

"Even if she caught him leaving one of those packages? I happen to know Mrs. Henderson, and she's one tough cookie. It's possible she laid into someone she found messing around in the alley. In a situation like that, can you say for sure that Matt wouldn't fight back?"

Liz sighed. "No. No, I cannot." She hesitated a moment, and then added, "I heard arguing upstairs last night after you left. But I couldn't tell what the conversation was about. And, I'm not sure, but one of the voices could have been Matt's."

"That's interesting," Jackson said. "Does he know any of the other guests?"

"He doesn't act as if he does. Portia is from the same area he is, so she seems the most likely person that he would know, but that might be a bit of a reach. They don't seem terribly chummy. Then again, I did find her wandering around on his floor. I don't know how suspicious that is, though. Lots of guests enjoy exploring all the inn's nooks and crannies."

"Does she seem like the curious type?"

Liz let out an indignant huff. "Only if she was making a list of things to complain about. Honestly, I have no idea why she's still here since she hates everything about this place. That alone seems suspicious to me. If I was that unhappy somewhere, I'd leave. But I don't want to label her a suspect just because I'm not keen on her. Matt seems much more likely. I'm pretty sure he's the one who left the newspapers for the guests in order to make problems for me."

"Newspapers?"

Liz explained about Rob Carver's front-page article and the newspapers that had mysteriously appeared at each guest's door. "I don't know if he's involved with the packages being left around town, but I'm fairly certain he's the source of the newspapers that frightened my guests this morning."

"I think it's time someone nudged the police in Matt's direction," Jackson said.

"I agree that he looks like the most probable culprit. The only thing that doesn't fit is that he got here *after* the first packages appeared."

"As far as you know. He could have been in the area well before he showed up on your doorstep. He's smart enough to be sure his arrival didn't coincide with these things."

"Matt's also a reporter," Liz said. "So he'd know how to create a big story that might turn me against Pleasant Creek . . . and vice versa."

"Sounds to me like we have a suspect."

Liz looked up as Sarah slipped back into the kitchen, the girl's eyes hopeful as she saw Liz on the phone. Liz held up one finger and smiled encouragingly. "Jackson, I need to go. I want to tell Sarah about Isaac. Then I'm planning to go check some of the local shops for the blue wrapping paper used in those packages."

Liz ended the call and then relayed to Sarah what Jackson had said about Isaac and Mrs. Henderson's condition. Sarah listened attentively as she spoke and then burst into tears.

"Are you all right?" Liz asked.

Sarah nodded fervently, wiping at her face. "I am so happy to hear that Mrs. Henderson will be all right and that Isaac isn't in any trouble."

Liz patted the young woman's shoulder gently. "Isaac is a good man. Everyone knows that. You needn't worry. From what Jackson said, you and Isaac are more heroes than suspects."

Sarah looked slightly alarmed at that. "We are not heroes. We would not want that kind of attention. It's unseemly."

"I don't think anyone is planning a parade," Liz said with a smile. "You'll be all right."

Sarah nodded soberly, oblivious to Liz's teasing. "I will go and clean upstairs now." She scurried out of the kitchen, and Liz fondly watched her go. Sarah was a serious girl, but she'd become very dear to Liz.

Liz considered finding Matt to talk to him about the newspapers and the arguing she'd overheard, but she didn't have the energy for that confrontation. She headed into Sew Welcome to chat with Mary Ann and Sadie before leaving on her search for the unusual blue paper. Though it was still a little early in the day for the shop's Christmas bustle, Liz did see her twin guests leafing through the pile of quilting fabrics that had been precut into fat quarters.

Gina peered over her glasses at Liz. "We're going to make some Christmas ornaments. Do you have any cookie cutters in the kitchen we could borrow?"

"Cookie cutters?" Liz wondered if the women were planning to make more applesauce dough.

"For patterns," Lois said. "We'll trace around them onto the fabric, and then sew and stuff them."

"They'll look adorable on the tree," Gina promised.

"On the tree here in the inn?" Liz asked.

Both of the women's heads bobbed in unison.

"Not to criticize," Lois said, "but it's still a little sparse, dear. We know you're going for a simple look, but I'm not sure you want it to be quite *that* simple."

"The storytelling in the sitting room is so much fun," Gina said. "We want the tree to look nice for everyone."

Liz looked back and forth between the two women, her eyes suddenly stinging with the threat of tears. "That's very kind of you. I'm so glad you aren't letting that horrible newspaper article drive you out of Pleasant Creek."

"Oh pishposh," Lois said. "We aren't going to let some sensational newspaper story scare us. So, do you have some cookie cutters? Maybe different shapes than the applesauce dough cookies?"

Liz sniffled slightly. "Yes, yes, I have lots of them in the kitchen.

I'll be happy to bring them to you. Where are you going to do your sewing?"

"You're welcome to work in here," Mary Ann said as she walked up to the ladies. She pointed at a long table in one corner where several portable sewing machines were lined up. "When we do classes, we use that space. But our classes are done for the holiday, so it's all yours."

Gina smiled at her. "That is so kind of you. We thought we might have to do them by hand."

"Which we could," Lois added, and her sister nodded. "But we can make a lot more ornaments with a machine." The two cheerful ladies carried a stack of fat quarters over to the shop register. Liz quickly told Sadie to put their purchases on her tab.

Mary Ann watched them with a fond smile. "It's nice when people surprise you in a good way, isn't it?"

"Thankfully, that happens a lot in Pleasant Creek," Liz said. "Otherwise the bad moments would be a little overwhelming."

"You mean the newspaper story?" Mary Ann asked.

"And the attack." At Mary Ann's surprised look, Liz realized that again she was forgetting who knew what. Dreadful events were piling up too fast. She dropped her voice and told Mary Ann about what had happened to Mrs. Henderson.

Mary Ann's eyes widened. "You need to tell Sadie," she whispered. "As soon as possible. She's known Doris Henderson since they were both in pigtails." She put a hand on Liz's arm. "I'll go get the cookie cutters for the ladies. I know where they are. You stay and tell Sadie."

Liz nodded as Mary Ann left. She watched Sadie regaling the two sisters with more extremely bad Christmas jokes.

"Why is Santa such a good gardener?" Sadie asked.

Gina grinned. "I know that one. Because he loves to hoe, hoe, hoe!"

Her sister groaned. "That was terrible."

Sadie led the twins over to the table and offered them a bag of scrap ribbon. "No cost," she said, speaking loud enough for Liz's benefit. "Since you're helping trim the tree that we all enjoy."

The sisters thanked her and began sorting through the ribbon eagerly.

Sadie walked over to Liz and said, "They're darling, both of them."

"They are," Liz said and then hesitated.

"What?" Sadie asked, catching onto Liz's discomfort right away. She gave Liz a teasing smile. "You're not going to ask me to stop telling Christmas jokes are you? I haven't gotten to my best stuff yet."

"No," Liz said quietly. "The jokes are fine. Well, actually, they're awful, but it's fine to tell them. I have some news about a friend of yours."

Sadie's smile faltered. "What kind of news?"

Liz told Sadie about the attack at Mama's Home Cooking, quickly adding that Jackson had said Mrs. Henderson was going to be fine.

Sadie paled as she listened, her stricken face contrasting sharply with the silly grinning Santa embroidered on her red sweater. "Doris's kids are always scolding her for going in all alone in the morning, but she never worried. She always said, 'What's going to happen in a nice town like Pleasant Creek?'"

Liz didn't answer that. They both knew that sometimes very unpleasant things happened in Pleasant Creek, but, still, it came as a shock every time. "At least she's going to be all right."

Sadie nodded. "I'm going over there as soon as Mary Ann comes back in here. I need to see her with my own eyes."

"Would you mind if I tag along?" Liz asked. "I want to hear Mrs. Henderson's account of the attack."

"Of course not." Sadie wrapped her arms around herself. "But Mary Ann said you were planning to go in search of the wrapping paper used in those packages."

"And I will. But I think your friend Doris is more important right now."

"I would certainly appreciate the company," Sadie said, suddenly looking older and far more serious than Liz ever remembered seeing her. "This Christmas isn't feeling so merry right now."

Liz didn't answer, as she had nothing to say to that. With the nasty Christmas surprises coming faster than snowflakes, she was terrified of what might happen next.

12

Within the first five minutes of being in Doris Henderson's hospital room, Liz could tell why she and Sadie were lifelong friends. Though gauze was wrapped around the restaurant owner's head, the face below the bandage wore the same wide smile as Sadie's when the two women saw each other. They were clearly kindred spirits.

"Why should you never eat your Christmas tree?" Sadie asked her friend in her usual booming voice.

"Because you'll get tinsel-itis!" Doris bellowed in response, barking out a laugh only to stop and put a hand to her head. "Stop! Laughing makes my head hurt."

"Just getting you back for scaring me nearly to death. I thought I was going to find you half dead in here. What were you doing in the alley by yourself at that time of morning?"

"My job," Doris retorted. "I heard a noise out back, and I went to see what it was." She pointed a finger at Sadie. "And don't go pretending you wouldn't have done the same thing, Sadie Schwarzentruber. I know you better than that."

"I might have *looked*. But I wouldn't have gotten close enough to get bonked in the head."

"Could you tell us exactly what happened?" Liz asked gently, before the conversation could grow heated.

Doris turned to her. "I don't know that I can. Some of it's a little blurry, but I remember opening the back door and seeing someone bent over with one of those packages. I yelled of course."

"How well did you see the person?"

"Not well. My son has been after me to install one of those

motion-activated security lights, but the expense never seemed worthwhile. Why would I need a security light? The only thing I ever get in that alley is the occasional raccoon."

"You never could listen to good advice," Sadie grumbled.

Doris turned to frown at her friend. "And how about you? I don't know how many times I had to tell you, 'Sadie, you ought to go out with that nice Schwarzentruber boy. He likes you.' But you always had an excuse."

Sadie scoffed. "I married him, didn't I?"

"Eventually." Doris crossed her arms over her ample chest. "And I would have put in the light. Eventually."

"Sure. Lock the barn door after the cow's gone."

Doris pursed her lips. "I do not see how the light would have made a difference."

"That's just it," Sadie snapped. "You couldn't see."

Before Doris could answer, Liz interrupted. "Could you tell if it was a man or a woman?"

Doris looked back at Liz, appearing startled by the question, and Liz was amused by the fact that Doris had clearly forgotten she was in the room. She supposed she probably did seem nearly invisible compared to the big personalities of Doris and Sadie.

After a moment, Doris said, "I think it was a man, but I'm not sure. It was someone about my height, and I'm six foot." She smiled. "There aren't a lot of women as tall as me. I tell my son I have Viking genes. Anyway, I stormed out and the back door swung almost shut, so it was pretty dark when the guy stood up. He ran at me and knocked me down. I must have hit my head then, because that's all I remember."

"I'm glad you've got a hard head," Sadie said.

"Hard enough," Doris agreed. "But the doctors won't let me out of here. I can't run a restaurant from this bed. And now I'll have hospital bills. Do they think I'm made of money?"

Barely hearing the two women chatter about bills, Liz thought about Matt. He was a little over six feet tall. She sighed. If height was the only clue that Doris could give them, it could just as easily have been Portia. The woman had to be nearly as tall as Matt, and she certainly seemed to have a grudge against Pleasant Creek and all its inhabitants. Portia hated everything about the place, but Liz could hardly picture her skulking around in a dark alley. She *could* picture her tackling someone, though.

Doris and Sadie launched back into Christmas jokes, booming out bad punch lines and laughing—though not without yelps of pain from Doris.

A young woman in neat powder blue scrubs and a name badge that identified her as Lucy walked in and frowned at them. "What is all the commotion in here?" she demanded. "This is a hospital, where people need rest and quiet."

Doris lifted her chin defiantly. "I don't need either of those things, so I don't belong in here."

Lucy crossed her arms. "That's not what the doctor says. You still have some scans scheduled." She turned to give Sadie a stern look. "And it doesn't help if visitors wind up our patients."

"Don't blame me," Sadie said. "Doris is self-winding. Always has been."

"All the same, I think she's had enough company for now."

"Don't I get a say in that?" Doris asked.

Lucy's gaze snapped to her. "No."

Liz spoke up then. "We should be going anyway. I need to get back to my guests at the inn." She smiled at Doris. "I'm glad to meet you and happy that you're recovering so well."

"I'll be back later today," Sadie said. "I'll bring you a care package."

Doris perked up at that. "Bring food. The stuff here is disgusting."

"Will do," Sadie promised as she and Liz slipped out the door.

Sadie's relief at finding her friend okay translated into her cracking more Christmas jokes on the way down the hospital hall. Though her jokes were terrible, the wildly wiggling eyes attached to the Santa face on her sweater made Liz laugh along with her much of the time. Despite Liz trying to signal a change in volume by keeping her own voice low, Sadie boomed out the punch lines loud enough to get glares from the nurses' station, but also the occasional chuckle from the rooms they passed.

When Liz and Sadie stepped into the elevator to return to the ground floor, they found two men in hospital scrubs already in the car. The men were talking about the same newspaper article that had upset the inn's guests that morning.

"My wife barely let me come to work today," one of the men said. "That article has her scared to death."

The other man grunted. "Sensationalized garbage."

"Maybe," said the first man. "But everyone's talking about it, and my wife isn't the only one who's afraid."

Not wanting to break in on a private conversation, Liz didn't say anything, but she did roll the men's words around in her head as she and Sadie drove back to the inn. It certainly seemed to her that if everyone was talking about the overblown article, it had accomplished at least some of what the reporter wanted. She wondered how badly Rob craved fame. Matt wasn't the only journalist capable of inventing a scary story for his own reasons. Rob was clearly benefiting from the arrival of the mysterious packages as well.

By the time they got back to the inn, Liz figured she'd heard every elementary-school Christmas joke in existence. She felt a headache coming on from the barrage of bad puns.

"You coming to the shop?" Sadie asked as they walked through the front door.

"Maybe later," Liz said. "I think I'll stop by the kitchen for a cup of coffee." *And a dose of aspirin.* She peeked through the sitting-room door before heading back to the kitchen. Already, a handful of simple fabric ornaments in bright calico prints hung from the tree. Liz recognized the shapes of the star in blue gingham and the red floral daisy from her cookie cutter collection. The sisters had been right—even the few additions brightened the tree considerably.

Despite her fear of more Christmas jokes, Liz headed into Sew Welcome in search of the twins to offer her gratitude. She found the sisters seated at the long table in the back of the room, stuffing white fiberfill into animal shapes. Liz gave them her warmest smile. "Those ornaments are adorable. Thank you so much. My favorite is the gingham star."

Both of the older women beamed at the praise. "I knew that star cookie cutter would make a nice ornament," Gina said. "Stars are so distinctive and Christmassy."

"I'm so grateful that you made them," Liz said. "They've transformed the tree."

"We've just started." Lois pointed to a pile of ornaments waiting to be stuffed. "We should have a dozen by this afternoon."

"Could you be a love and get us another card of small black buttons?" Gina asked. "Mary Ann knows the ones we need." She held up the lightly stuffed ornament in her hands. "I need them to make eyes for this kitty."

"I'll be happy to." Liz walked over to the counter and relayed the request.

"They've been working all morning," Mary Ann said softly as she handed Liz the card of buttons. "All that industry almost makes me feel lazy."

"I feel guilty that they're using part of their holiday for the tree here," Liz said.

"Don't worry about it. They're clearly happy as clams."

Liz was handing over the card of buttons to the sisters when the shop door opened. She turned and was surprised to see Jackson wave at her from the doorway.

"Oh," Gina said. "Is that your boyfriend? He's very handsome."

"No," Lois corrected. "Her boyfriend is that nice-looking young man who is staying here. Don't you remember?"

"Well, she might have more than one boyfriend," Gina said with a sniff. "I always did."

"You did not."

"That's the mayor," Liz informed them gently, feeling her cheeks warm at the twins' analysis of her love life.

"A mayor." Lois gave Liz a wink. "Good choice."

Liz wasn't certain what to say in response to that. Jackson wasn't her boyfriend, and Matt definitely wasn't, but at least she and Jackson were friends. And she suspected they could possibly be more than friends someday, though who could see the future? At one time she'd been certain she was going to marry Matt and look at how dreadfully that had turned out.

"Liz?" Jackson had crossed the room while she was frozen in her tracks after being flustered by the twins.

"Good morning, Mr. Mayor," Gina spoke up. "Merry Christmas."

Jackson turned a warm smile to the older woman. "Thank you. Merry Christmas to you. Are you both staying here at the inn?"

"We are," Lois said. "It's lovely, and Liz is such a wonderful innkeeper and so pretty. Don't you think so?"

Jackson's eyebrows raised at the oddly phrased question. "She is a fine innkeeper and a lovely person," he said smoothly. "Pleasant Creek is lucky to have her."

"I'm sure," Gina said as she leaned toward her sister and giggled. Lois joined in, and Liz felt her cheeks warm even more.

"You'll need to excuse the mayor and me," Liz said to them before they could embarrass her further. "Thank you again for the ornaments."

"Happy to help." Lois flapped a hand at them. "You two run along."

As Liz and Jackson walked out of the fabric shop, he gave her a wry smile. "I got the feeling there was a whole conversation going on there that I missed."

"I'd rather not talk about it," Liz said as they strode past the stairs and into the kitchen. "I assume you're here about the packages?"

"The chief called me this morning. He said the teeth were definitely from a child and had come out on their own. The bones weren't human. They came from a cat."

"That's a relief. Anything about the blood on the glass shard? That *was* blood, right?"

He nodded. "Human blood. On the glass from your package and from the one found at the restaurant this morning. It's old and badly degraded, but it's human."

Liz walked to the coffeemaker and busied her hands with fixing coffee for both of them. "So the glass was used to hurt someone?"

"Probably not," Jackson said as he leaned on the counter next to Liz. "It was windshield glass. If it was broken in an accident, the blood could have gotten on it then."

"Maybe that's some kind of sick clue. Is the chief checking into old car crashes in Pleasant Creek?"

"He is, but even in a quiet area like Pleasant Creek, there have been a lot of auto accidents."

"If the packages are in response to an accident," Liz said, "I imagine it must have been a bad one. That should help narrow it down."

"Some. The chief told me he's considering the possibility that the glass is from an accident that was never reported. Perhaps this is some strange way of pointing us toward an undiscovered crash. With blood this old and degraded, it's probably a reach. We have a few remote areas around here, but hiding a wrecked car would be difficult. There are no deep culverts that could conceal an auto accident, especially for years. Still, the chief has sent officers to scout around some of the more secluded locations. It'll take time."

While he was speaking, Mary Ann had slipped into the kitchen. When he'd finished, she asked, "Accidents and blood? That all sounds so grisly."

Jackson nodded. "This package business is turning more serious by the day."

"Other than the blood on the glass, there's nothing else in the package that provides any clues, correct?" Liz asked. "How about the teddy bear head?"

"It was from a fairly pricy toy made by a German company and discontinued about fifteen years ago. It was old, but not particularly rare. And the cloth strips were simple cotton flannel, so nothing unusual there." Jackson stopped and took a sip of the coffee Liz had handed him.

"Do you think I could see a piece of the cloth?" Mary Ann asked. "I keep hearing about it, but I haven't seen any of it up close. I know a lot about fabric. Maybe if I saw it, I could help."

Jackson's expression suggested doubt, but he still told Mary Ann he'd ask the chief about getting a piece. "It might be difficult. Once something is checked into evidence, they don't exactly pass it around to the public."

"I understand. I would like to do something to help, though," Mary Ann said. "With Doris in the hospital, this is all getting a little too frightening. I want to feel as if I'm doing something besides waiting for another package to be delivered or another friend to be hurt."

"Of course." Jackson turned back to Liz. "Speaking of checking up on the parts of the package, I assume you haven't tracked down the wrapping paper yet?"

"I haven't even started," Liz confessed. "I wanted to check on Mrs. Henderson at the hospital and talk to her first."

"It's probably a long shot anyway."

Just then they heard a series of deep barks from the foyer. Liz exchanged glances with Jackson, and they both ran for the doorway.

Anything that could get that much response from Beans had to be bad. Really bad.

13

By the time Liz and Jackson reached the foyer, the barking had turned to growling. Liz saw Matt plastered against one of the walls, the cuff of his pants in Beans's jaw. The bulldog had all four legs braced so he could shake his head with the fabric in his mouth.

"It's attacking me!" Matt yelled. "It's gone rabid. Kill it! Kill it!"

Rolling her eyes at Matt's melodramatic shouts, Liz bent down to grab the bulldog's collar, never an easy task since it required feeling around his loose flaps of skin until she found it. "Come on, big boy," she said, hauling the dog backward. "Let go of the naughty man."

Beans cheerfully released his mouthful of pant leg, leaving behind a thick coating of drool. He looked up at Liz adoringly, his stump of a tail wagging. She fought down a laugh and scratched between the dog's ears.

"That mutt needs to be put down." Matt wiped the sweat from his brow. "Look at my pants."

He moaned over his expensive slacks while Liz dragged the dog across the floor to where Jackson was standing with a wide smile on his face.

"Hold on to him, will you?" she asked.

"Sure." Jackson knelt down and began petting Beans, who sighed happily. "Good dog. You're such a good dog."

"Beans seems to think you're a threat," Liz said as she straightened back up and turned to face Matt again.

"I'm not responsible for what that crazy mutt thinks."

"No, you're not," Liz said. "But you are responsible for sneaking around outside in the dark."

"I explained that—"

Liz held up a hand to stop his rebuttal. "And you were upstairs arguing with someone in the middle of the night as well. Plus, I know you're the one who left newspapers for everyone to find this morning. What exactly are you doing here, Matt? Besides making my life miserable and giving my dog indigestion?"

"You know why I'm here. I want you to come to Boston and spend Christmas with me."

Liz shook her head. "You don't care about us getting back together. I'm not stupid. You haven't been pining away for me, and I certainly haven't been longing for you. I want to know what's going on. And try and make it the truth this time."

Matt shook his head. "This suspicious streak is so unlike you. See what this place is doing to you?"

"Tell me what's going on," Liz repeated. "Spill it, or I'm going to knock you down and let Beans chew your nose off the way he did with my plastic Santa."

Matt looked from Jackson to Mary Ann and Sadie, who had come to investigate the noise. "All of you heard her threaten me."

"Yes," Jackson said. "And I'll help hold you down. I'm pretty sure Beans hasn't had dinner yet."

"Normally I'm opposed to violence," Mary Ann said mildly. "But there are exceptions to every rule."

"I'm never really against violence," Sadie added. "And if you're the guy who attacked my friend this morning, I'll buy Beans a present for biting you."

"Attacked your friend?" Matt blinked, clearly confused. "I didn't attack anyone. I don't know what you're talking about." He turned to look at Liz. "You aren't telling people I attacked you?"

Liz stepped closer to look directly into Matt's face. "The owner of a local restaurant caught someone leaving a package in the alley, and she was knocked down and ended up in the hospital because of it. What do you have to do with these packages, Matt?"

"Nothing." Matt shook his head adamantly. "I put out the newspapers this morning, sure, but I didn't *cause* the news story. That's all on this freaky town you've moved to."

"You seem awfully set on convincing Liz that Pleasant Creek is bad," Mary Ann said. "You have to know how guilty that makes you look."

Matt's face took on a stubborn frown, and he crossed his arms over his chest. "I didn't do anything wrong."

"I don't believe you." Liz poked him in the chest to emphasize each word.

Matt looked from one accusing face to another and then leaned toward Liz and dropped his voice. "Honestly, all I want is for you to come back for the Sheridan family Christmas party. That's it. I swear."

"Why would you possibly want that?"

Matt's defensive posture deflated, and he ran his hand through his hair, mussing his normally perfect style. "You know that my grandfather likes you—better than he likes me, even."

"There's a shock," Jackson muttered, and Sadie snorted with laughter.

"So? Mr. Sheridan is a sweet old gentleman." Liz crossed her arms.

Matt huffed and pointed at Beans, who was quietly drooling on Jackson's shoe. "Sweet? My grandfather is more of an attack dog than that mutt."

"He's always been kind to me," Liz said.

"Exactly. He loves you. And his doctor says his heart condition is getting worse. He's not going to last much longer. As long as you're in my life, I know I'm not written out of his will, so if you could pretend to still be my girlfriend, or maybe my fiancée, just for the holidays . . ."

"You want me to *lie* to a dying man?" Liz enunciated each word with a mix of scorn and disbelief in her voice.

"Not a *big* lie—more of an implied lie. You'd be making him happy." Matt gave her his most charming smile. "I know how much you enjoy making people happy."

"You know, every time I think you couldn't possibly stoop any lower, you surprise me," Liz said. "I'd call you a snake, but that would be degrading to snakes. I am *not* going to help you con a sick old man."

"Look," Matt dropped his voice again, "I'm willing to pay you. You can't tell me that as an innkeeper you couldn't use a few extra bucks. When the will is settled, I'll give you a percentage of whatever the old man leaves me. That's fair."

"Can we get Beans to bite him again?" Sadie interjected.

"I don't think that's a good idea," Mary Ann answered. "He's liable to get food poisoning."

"It might be worth it," Jackson said, gently pushing Beans off his shoe. The dog snorted and waddled over to his favorite rug to flop back down. He was clearly done with all the drama.

"You know, this doesn't exactly clear you from being the one who knocked down Mrs. Henderson and caused her to hit her head," Liz said. "It only means you have a strong motive to make me fear staying in Pleasant Creek over Christmas. A motive more than strong enough to make you leave those disgusting packages."

Matt held up his hands. "No. I haven't done anything illegal. I wouldn't. I'm a reporter, and I know where the line is. Besides, weren't some of those packages delivered before I even got here? I couldn't exactly have been making deliveries while I was in Boston."

"I know when you *appeared* to get here," Liz said. "But that doesn't prove anything. You could have been in the area for days before I saw you. This isn't the only place to stay in the county. A man who would defraud his own grandfather certainly wouldn't draw the line at stuffing a few boxes with rags and hay."

"I didn't do it! Call the paper. They'll verify I was in Boston."

"Maybe we should call Chief Houghton," Jackson suggested. "He can figure out exactly where you were when the packages began showing up here."

"You don't need to call anyone," a female voice said from the doorway. "I can tell you exactly where he was."

14

Every face turned to the doorway where Portia Brecken stood, looking at them with her usual disdainful smirk.

"How is that?" Liz asked.

Portia's laser glare pinpointed Liz. "He was with me."

"Why was he with you?"

"Because I'm his fiancée."

"Oh this is good," Sadie said. "I wish I had popcorn."

Liz ignored her chuckling friend and turned to scowl at Matt. "You have a fiancée? Why would you want me to pretend to be your fiancée when you already have one?"

Matt shrugged. "Portia's not exactly a people person."

"You think?" Sadie asked with a hoot of laughter. "We've got bobcats around here that are cuddlier than her."

Liz gave Sadie a sharp look. "Could you please let me handle this?"

Totally unabashed, Sadie mimed turning a key at her lips. "I won't say another word."

I'll believe that when I see it. Liz returned her attention to Matt and poked him in the chest again, this time hard enough to get a yelp in response. "You not only want me to con your grandfather, you were trying to con me. How *dare* you pretend you want to get back together when you have a fiancée? What if I'd actually believed you?"

"I would have come up with some reason why we couldn't stay together after Christmas."

For that, Liz gave him another poke. "Jerk!"

He yelped again. "That hurts!"

"Good," Liz said. "So, why is Portia here in Pleasant Creek? To help you pack boxes with rags and dead mice?"

Portia laughed. When Liz turned to look at her, she shrugged one elegant shoulder. "You can't possibly be suggesting *I* would touch a dead animal."

"She's pretty tall," Sadie said, sizing up the haughty woman. "In the dark, Doris might have mistaken her for a man."

"That is the most ridiculous thing I have ever heard," Portia said. "Not even one of you hillbillies could possibly mistake me for a man."

"Portia and I aren't conspiring to do anything. I didn't even want her here," Matt insisted. Liz looked at him in surprise. "I was shocked to find her already checked into the inn when I arrived. I thought she was staying behind in Boston."

"Then why *is* she here?" Liz asked. When Matt didn't respond, she turned to Portia for an answer.

Portia glared back for a moment, but finally gave in. "I came to Pleasant Creek to make sure Matt didn't let any old feelings detour him from his goal." She sniffed. "But that was before I met you, obviously. If I'd known we were coming to Green Acres, I wouldn't have bothered."

"You should have seen Liz when she was a lawyer in Boston," Matt said. "She was breathtaking."

Jackson narrowed his eyes at Matt. "You're really not helping yourself."

"I think I'll pass on imagining your ex as breathtaking," Portia said with a roll of her eyes. She returned her attention to Liz. "Matthew is not the most trustworthy of fiancés, so I thought it best to keep an eye on him. I have invested a fair amount of time in our relationship, and I don't want him getting any foolish romantic notions about you."

"Why are you engaged to him if you don't trust him?" Liz asked.

Portia waved her hand as if brushing away a minor detail. "Our relationship is based on mutual benefit. Mutual trust isn't necessary . . . or wise. We will both profit from our marriage."

Liz smiled tightly. "You just need to get past his family first."

The woman gave a single small nod. "I admit I struggle with the kind of doglike friendliness that seems to come so naturally to you."

At that, Sadie burst out in a fit of laughter. "*Dog*like friendliness?" Every eye turned to her, but it took the hooting woman a moment to catch her breath. Finally she managed to explain. "It's so rich, don't you see? It was the dog attacking Matt that brought us in here in the first place. So we've come full circle."

Though Liz found little about the circumstances funny, she did see Sadie's point concerning the absurdity of the whole situation. And as she looked between Portia's disapproving scowl and Matt's beseeching eyes, she just couldn't picture them as a villainous duo secretly handing out the mysterious packages. In fact, she couldn't see the two of them acting together well in any scheme. They clearly had simpler—and more self-serving—goals.

Liz turned back to Matt. "It must be clear to you by now that I am not coming back to Boston. For Christmas or any other time."

"If it's a matter of expense . . ." Matt began, but snapped his mouth shut at Liz's icy stare.

"You don't understand me at all. Go back to Boston. Let your family meet Portia. Who knows? Maybe they'll love her, as unlikely as that seems."

"I suppose I could tell the old man that you're sick and couldn't come this year," Matt said thoughtfully. "He could be gone before the next family event."

Liz shook her head. "No. In fact, I'm going to give him a call to make sure he's up to date on my life. So I recommend you don't tell him any lies about me."

"You wouldn't."

"I most certainly will."

Matt turned and dashed out of the foyer.

Liz assumed he intended to make the phone call before she could beat him to it, but she shouted after him, "Be sure to pack while you're up there!"

The only response was the sound of his feet on the steps.

"Don't worry," Portia said. "I believe we've spent more than enough time in this horrible little village. I'll see to it that we're in Boston before the mud from this bumpkin town can dry on my boots. They cost a fortune, and I don't want them ruined." She followed Matt up the stairs at a more sedate pace.

"I don't believe I've ever met a couple who deserved each other more," Sadie said. She turned to look down at Beans lying on his rug. "Now, I'm going to go get *you* a doggie treat."

Jackson walked over to stand beside Liz. "They certainly gave us a show, but I don't think they had anything to do with the packages. You know him better than I do, though. What do you think?"

Liz sighed. "I agree. It's hard to imagine that they're the ones responsible. I had really hoped we might have solved it." She turned to smile at Jackson. "At the same time, any encounter that ends with those two leaving my inn can't be all bad."

Jackson departed not long after, remarking that he needed to swing by Cross Furniture Company before checking in again with the chief. Liz walked him to the door and then headed back to the kitchen to whip up some treats for the evening's social hour in the sitting room.

Sarah met her in the short hallway outside the kitchen. The quiet young woman gave Liz a wan smile. "Do you want me to help with the guest social tonight, Miss Eckardt? I owe you some extra time since I came in so late this morning."

Liz shook her head. "You don't have to make up for that time.

You were late because you were needed elsewhere. I understand that. Besides, I think the group will be smaller tonight. Arthur has plans with Mary Ann, some folks have tickets for the candlelight tour of homes, and two of our guests are leaving."

Sarah's eyes widened. "They are? It is not because of the newspaper article, is it? I heard some of the guests talking about it."

"No, though I could certainly have done without that. Mr. Sheridan and Miss Brecken are leaving tonight."

"I could stay and clean their rooms," Sarah offered.

"You can clean them in the morning. We aren't expecting any new guests tomorrow. Is Isaac coming for you?"

Sarah bobbed her head. "He is, but if you want me to clean the rooms, Isaac will not mind waiting."

"Really, there's no need. Tomorrow is soon enough. Drive carefully and get home safely, and I'll be happy."

"Thank you. I'll tidy the kitchen a little and go." Sarah gave her such a sweet smile that Liz felt her spirits lift.

It had been a tough day, but certainly no harder for Liz than for Sarah. If the young woman could find the grace to smile, so could Liz. She followed the girl into the kitchen to whip up something chocolate to celebrate Matt and Portia's departure.

———————————————————

After night had fallen, bringing a deep chill along with it, Liz hurried to the sitting room to build a welcoming fire. The Sheltons strolled in just as she finished. Mrs. Shelton's hand was tucked into the crook of her husband's arm and his fingers rested over hers.

Liz smiled at the sweet couple. "I'll have some treats out in a moment."

The pair settled down on the sofa, and Mrs. Shelton pulled the edges of her pale gray cardigan tighter around her.

Her husband noticed at once. "Are you cold?"

"A little," his wife admitted. "The fire will warm me in a minute."

"I'll get you a jacket." Mr. Shelton hurried out of the room before his wife could protest.

She watched him go fondly and then turned to Liz. "Will we be the only guests enjoying the sitting room tonight?"

"I believe so," Liz said. "The candlelight tour has been quite a draw."

Mrs. Shelton's lined face looked wistful. "I would have enjoyed that."

"Were you not able to get tickets?"

Mrs. Shelton shook her head sadly. "It wasn't that. I tire easily these days, and the nights are too cold for me. I haven't been well."

"I'm so sorry to hear that."

"I'm going to begin a course of treatment after the holidays, though it's one of those times when the cure is worse than the disease, at least for a while. That's why we're here. I wanted to have a nice, romantic Christmas before going back to face reality."

Mr. Shelton came in at the end of his wife's remark and tucked a sweater around her with a worried frown. He turned to Liz. "I hope there aren't going to be any more shouting matches at the inn. It's really not good for Judy."

"There won't be," Liz promised him. "The rest of your visit should be peaceful. And to that end, let me go and get my magic chocolate dream bars. I guarantee they'll erase any unpleasantness from the day."

"I believe that is exactly the medicine I need," Mrs. Shelton said, smiling.

As Liz retrieved the treats from the kitchen, she hoped that what she'd told her guests would prove true. *At least tonight will be drama free,* Liz reassured herself as she headed back to the sitting room bearing the tray.

Moments later the front door creaked open unexpectedly and an icy wind blasted her in the foyer. *What now?*

15

Liz struggled not to drop the tray of chocolate cookie bars as she turned to see who was coming in the door. When she saw the smiling face of Charlie, she nearly groaned aloud. In the craziness of her day, she'd completely forgotten about the storyteller.

"I'll be right with you, Charlie," Liz called before rushing into the sitting room and setting the tray on the low table in front of the love seat the Sheltons snuggled on. "The storyteller is here. Would you two care to hear a story tonight?" Liz practically held her breath, afraid that the couple would rather sit together alone by the fire.

Mrs. Shelton's face lit up. "I've been looking forward to it all day, but I was afraid he might not come since the two of us are the only audience."

He probably wouldn't have if someone had called him. Liz held on to her smile. "I'm sure he'll be happy to tell you a story. I'll go get him." She returned to the foyer and found Charlie where she had left him.

Charlie looked at her expectantly. "Is everyone ready in the sitting room?"

"Actually, I kind of forgot you were coming." Liz winced at the disappointment that quickly filled his face. "Which doesn't mean we don't want you. It's only that most of the guests are at the candlelight tour of homes. So you'll be speaking to one couple and me. I will, of course, still pay your full fee."

For a moment, a frown crossed the young man's face, but then his open smile reappeared. "I love a big audience, of course, but I'll be happy to tell a story for whoever is here." Then some darker emotion flickered in his eyes, vanishing before Liz could identify it. "Please, tell me one of the two people I'll be speaking to isn't the guy who hated last night's story."

Liz raised her hands. "No, I wouldn't do that to you. He has checked out."

"Then I'm ready whenever you are."

Liz led the way to the sitting room, and the Sheltons greeted Charlie warmly.

"The story you told last night was so uplifting," Mrs. Shelton said.

The storyteller thanked her and took his place close to the crackling fire. Liz grabbed a chocolate cookie bar from the serving platter and perched on one of the two wing chairs.

Charlie looked across the faces of his tiny audience and launched into his story. "Snow fell fast and wild on a dark Christmas Eve. A young couple drove through the worsening storm, their car headlights turning each flake into sparkling confetti against the black night. The wind blew the flakes in swirls and eddies, making visibility nearly zero. In the backseat, a small boy slept, worn out and already wearing his warm, cozy pajamas so his father might simply carry him into the house when they arrived home. *If* they arrived home."

Liz realized she'd leaned forward as she listened. The story took a dark turn when the car slid on an icy patch of road and struck a tree. Liz was grateful that Charlie didn't add any gory details to that part. She wondered why he had chosen such a dreary story before she remembered Matt hassling the young storyteller about his happy tale the night before. *Thanks, Matt.*

She looked hesitantly toward the Sheltons. Mrs. Shelton was clearly mesmerized, her concerned eyes fixed on the young man telling the story. Her husband was already frowning slightly and stealing glances at his wife.

Please let this have a happy ending.

"The little boy woke as the car grew cold," Charlie said. "And in the darkness, he couldn't see anyone. He called for his parents, but got no answer, so he pushed open the car door and padded out into the storm, leaving the car and his family behind."

Liz felt a stab of panic. *What kind of Christmas story is this?*

"The child walked and walked, lost and afraid, until he spotted a flickering light. He followed it to a barn where an Amish farmer was settling his animals for the night. The man took one look at the shivering child and bundled him in his own coat. He carried the boy into his house. His wife quickly changed the child into dry pajamas from her own son's clothes and warmed him before the fire."

Liz glanced toward the Sheltons again and saw their expressions had not changed. At least Charlie's story had brought the child out of the cold. The tale continued with the boy falling asleep while the farmer went back into the snow to look for the child's parents. The storm worsened and the Amish wife stared out at the falling flakes, waiting for her husband to return.

"As the wife stood before the window, speaking quietly to Gött in her heart, she heard a small voice. It was the child, praying his own prayer," Charlie said. He dropped to one knee and his voice grew soft, imitating a child speaking. "'You can have all of my presents under the tree, even my Mighty Marvin Power Patrol set that I know Santa must have brought because it was in my letter. You can have them all, because that's not what I want for Christmas anymore. I just want my mom and dad.'"

Liz blinked against the tears in her eyes, strongly affected by Charlie's portrayal of the small child's need and faith.

"Eventually," Charlie continued, "the little boy fell asleep, bundled in quilts on a pallet before the fire. Snow continued to fall throughout the night. The boy did not wake until morning when light filled the farmhouse and the Amish children rushed downstairs to look shyly at the stranger and ask their Mutter what had happened." Charlie changed his voice for each of the children asking about their father.

"Though sick with worry," Charlie continued, his voice quiet, "the wife showed none of it to her children. 'When Gött brings him home, he will be home.'"

Liz nearly began fidgeting in her seat as she remembered Matt harassing Charlie about how every story had to have a happy ending. Surely he wasn't going to finish the story with death. She gasped with relief when the Amish farmer finally burst through the farmhouse door, shaking snow from his clothes, the boy's battered parents behind him.

Mrs. Shelton clapped her hands when the little boy and his parents were reunited. "That was wonderful," she said. "I was so nervous as you were telling it."

"I imagine that was the plan," her husband said.

After he spoke with the Sheltons for a few minutes, Charlie headed back out to the foyer and Liz went with him.

"I have to admit, you had me worried," she said. "I thought maybe Matt's criticism last night had inspired you a little too much in your choice of story, but that was very touching."

"Thank you. A good story has to get all the characters in as much trouble as possible before it digs them out." He dropped his voice slightly. "I have to admit, this story was inspired by the things going on in Pleasant Creek right now."

"Going on?" Liz echoed, though she immediately made the connections herself since Jackson had said the glass in some of the packages was almost certainly from a car accident.

"The packages." He gazed at her with curiosity. "You do know about them? It seems as though everyone I meet is talking about who has gotten one and what's inside."

"Yes, I know about them," Liz said. "I guess I don't like thinking about such terrible things this time of year."

Charlie looked sheepish. "I read about them in the newspaper this morning too. That reporter clearly relishes the whole macabre business."

Then he shrugged. "I don't suppose I have any right to throw stones though, since I did use the newspaper story to inspire my tale tonight."

"You made that story up today?" Liz was surprised. "You're very talented."

Charlie smiled. "Thank you." As they talked, Beans had lifted himself from his snoozing spot on the rug and shuffled over to snuffle at the storyteller's pants. "Maybe I should come up with a story about a bulldog who saves the day."

"Unless he saves it by drooling on someone, Beans wouldn't be a great model."

Charlie cleared his throat. "Will you want me back tomorrow night?"

"I think so." Liz walked over to pick up one of her business cards from a holder on a nearby table. "Could you ring me in the afternoon so we can be sure? I would promise to call you, but I'm beginning to forget my head in the Christmas rush."

"I don't mind calling," Charlie said. "I'll talk to you tomorrow."

As Charlie turned to go, the front door opened and Rob burst in. The reporter paid no attention to the storyteller and merely pointed at Liz as he approached her. "I want to talk to you."

"I do *not* want to talk to you," Liz said. Charlie eased around them and headed for the door. She gave the storyteller a wave and then faced her unexpected company. Beans sat between Liz and Rob, looking up at each of them. Liz took a step closer to the reporter, sidestepping the dog. "I don't appreciate how much your ridiculous article frightened my guests."

"It wasn't ridiculous," Rob said. "It was information people need to know, and you cannot suppress it."

"I'm not trying to suppress anything," Liz insisted. "But I also don't see any need to inflate it."

"Actually, I heard you *are* suppressing information. I got a phone call today from an anonymous source saying you were doing exactly that, keeping important facts from the public. So what do you know?"

Liz fumed, assuming Matt was making trouble again. "I am not a source of secret information. Anything I know, you could find out from annoying the police or the mayor, and probably get more details while you're at it."

"I don't believe you."

"I don't care what you believe. I also don't want to be quoted in any more of your articles. Plenty of business owners have received packages since we did. Any of those people would be a better source than me."

Beans had been pointedly shifting his attention between Rob and Liz as they spoke. Apparently he finally made a decision as he hefted himself to his feet, walked the few steps to the reporter, and sat on the man's foot.

Rob gave the dog a passing glance, pulling his shoe out from under his furry rump. "So, cotton rags, dead mouse, cat bones, windshield glass, and hay," he said. "Nothing else? The police aren't holding any information back?"

"If they are, they aren't sharing it with me." Liz waved her hands in exasperation. "There's no conspiracy. If there was, I can't see any reason they'd include me in it."

The reporter raised an eyebrow. "It seems to me that you'd have access to information considering your *special* relationship with the mayor." His pointed, snarky tone was slightly marred by an annoyed glance down. Beans had again taken a seat on Rob's shoe.

Liz was disgusted at his insinuation. "I'm not even going to dignify that with a response."

Both Liz and the reporter jumped in surprise as the bulldog snorted and belched with startling volume. The reporter's face reflected pure repulsion as he pulled his foot out from under the dog's rump again.

"You know," Rob said, his tone a bit distracted as he continued to eye Beans. "It's better if you give me a statement."

"Better for you, maybe."

At that, Beans shook his head vigorously, slinging ropes of slobber through the air. Liz winced when a small bit struck the bottom of her corduroy slacks, but the bulk of the mess spattered against the reporter's leg.

That clearly was the limit even for a man as persistent as Rob. He backed away toward the door. "I'm not done."

"Beans probably isn't, either," Liz said.

With a huff, the man spun on his heel and marched out the door. Liz reached down to pat Beans on the head. "Some days, I truly love you." Beans responded with a wheeze and licked her hand.

After a quick peek into the sitting room, where the Sheltons sat close together and talked softly before the fire, Liz headed for the kitchen. She decided to have a soothing cup of tea and leaf through some cookbooks to plan a wonderful Christmas Eve breakfast for her guests. She'd put off making her changes to the menu long enough and finally needed to replace all of her godson's favorites with something just as special. She shook off the wave of sadness as she thought of Steve, so far from home at Christmastime.

Liz was sipping cherry vanilla tea when she heard the front door open. She walked out to greet her guests as they returned from the candlelight tour.

"It was perfect," Vivian gushed. "The homes were beautiful."

"Gina and I got great ideas for decorating," Lois said, and her sister bobbed her head in agreement. "I'm so glad we went."

Liz listened to more cheerful chatter before the guests headed upstairs for the night. Then she locked up and walked back to the kitchen to drink the last bit of tea in her mug.

She had finished and was rinsing out the mug when Beans ambled through the kitchen door and shuffled over to his water dish. She saw something trailing from the dog's slobbery jowls.

"What have you picked up now?" she asked. With Beans's tendency to drool copiously, he was equally prone to dragging things into the house when they stuck to his goopy jowls.

Liz walked across the room and plucked a piece of cloth from the dog's chin. It was a strip of old flannel, grayed with mold. Liz looked at the material curiously. She recognized it as being identical to the scraps of fabric she'd seen in the mysterious packages.

The question was: How had Beans gotten it?

16

As Beans turned back to slurp up more water, Liz stood over him with the limp scrap of fabric in her hand. "Where did you get this thing, buddy?"

If Beans had an answer, he wasn't telling. Liz thought back to the two packages that had been found at the inn. Although Beans had torn paper from the corner of the first package, he hadn't ripped through to the inside where the cloth scraps had been. And the police had been diligent in collecting every bit of fabric and hay from her package as well as the one left at Sew Welcome. Still, if the soggy piece of flannel hadn't come from one of the packages, where would Beans have gotten it?

Beans had the run of the inn, but the rotund bulldog certainly didn't casually climb to the upper floors; it wasn't likely he got it from any of the guest rooms. Granted, fabric tended to cling. If one of the guests was putting together the packages in the inn, a scrap might have stuck to their clothes and been transferred to the bulldog somehow.

As she thought about clothes, she pictured Beans tugging Matt's pant leg. What if the fabric was caught in the cuff of Matt's slacks? By the time he left, he'd managed to convince her that he was innocent—of the package prank at least—but he'd fooled her before. He could have been lying the whole time.

To be fair, Beans *had* showed interest in both Charlie and Rob as well, even if the bulldog had been far less hostile to them than he had been to Matt. And Rob was milking the story of the mysterious packages for all it was worth. If he truly thought reporting on those packages could be his golden ticket out of Pleasant Creek, he had as much motive as Matt. Certainly both reporters wanted to use the boxes to their own advantage, but was either actually responsible for them?

She turned the scrap over and over in her hands. Rob was the last person Beans had interacted with. But Matt was the one the dog had actually tugged at. She spun the possibilities in her mind until, finally, each of the men felt equally suspect. Clutching the rag in one hand, Liz decided to call Jackson and tell him what she'd found. Hopefully he could help her gain some clarity.

Liz sighed in frustration when she got Jackson's voice mail. She glanced toward the clock on the wall and grimaced. It was a little late to make calls. With a sigh, she folded up the fabric scrap and slipped it into a plastic bag. She put it in a drawer, intending to forget about it until morning.

After flipping through two cookbooks with no memory of a single recipe, Liz had to face facts. The moldy material was going to worry her all night unless she managed to do something about it. Even one step toward finding out who'd left it would make her feel better. And since there was only one person on her short list of suspects she felt comfortable calling and disturbing, she quickly dialed Matt's cell number.

He answered on the last ring before the call rolled to voice mail. "Liz, what?"

"You don't sound very cheery. Did I wake you?"

"No," he snapped. "I had a big fight with Portia on the plane, thanks to you."

"My good deed for the day. I need to ask you something."

"If you've changed your mind about coming to Boston, forget it. I already 'fessed up to my grandfather. He took it about as well as you'd expect and called me an idiot for losing you."

"You can't imagine I'd argue with that assessment."

"No, you and the old man always were on the same wavelength," Matt grumbled. "So is that why you called? To rub it in?"

"No, I found something. Beans was dragging around a piece of cloth like the stuff that has been turning up in the packages, and since he was chewing on you . . ."

"I can't believe you're still accusing me of that. I told you, Liz, I had nothing to do with those packages."

"You just took advantage of them for your own gain."

"I saw an opportunity. I seized it. But I didn't create it."

"I want to believe you," Liz said, though that was a total lie. She didn't actually want to believe him. She wanted him to be the culprit because she wasn't afraid of Matt. If he was guilty, the boxes would be simply disgusting and wrong, but not overtly menacing.

"I didn't leave them. I was in Boston when all that started."

"So you say."

"Actually, I have someone who can verify it other than my boss," Matt said. "Portia insisted on dinner at the priciest place in town before I left. It's her favorite spot, and they know me. You can call them, and they'll tell you that Portia and I were there the night before I left for Indiana. I couldn't be in two places at once, so that should settle it." He told Liz the name of the restaurant and read out the phone number from his contacts list.

"I will check this out, you know."

"Fine. I don't want to fight with you anymore."

Liz paused. She didn't want to prolong the call, but there was one thing she knew to be true. Matt was devious, but he was also smart and a reporter. If he wasn't the one who left the packages, he might have an idea who did. "One more thing—"

"Great." His voice dripped with sarcasm. "What?"

"You read the article in the newspapers you left for the guests."

"Yeah. It wasn't bad work. A little overblown, but not bad."

"I'm sure the scumbag who wrote it would be pleased you approve," Liz said dryly. "Apparently he's hoping this story will be the springboard that launches him from a small-town paper to the big time."

"You can't blame him for that."

Liz ignored the comment, feeling she could definitely reproach Rob for throwing local businesses under the bus at Christmastime to further his own goals, but she didn't want to debate journalism ethics with another reporter. "Fine. What I want to know is whether he might be manufacturing the story as well as reporting on it."

"Oh." Matt paused, clearly thinking about it. "That would be a huge risk. If he got caught, he would probably lose his job there and mark himself as damaged goods for any other newspaper. It would be career suicide."

"So you don't think he'd do it."

"I didn't say that. It would depend on how desperate the man is to get out of Pleasant Creek. I could see how he might be willing to take the risk. That town is certainly the last place I'd want to spend the rest of my life."

Liz sighed. "So you'd consider him a suspect."

"A better one than me, since I *didn't do it*." Matt emphasized the last three words with increasing volume, and then he hung up.

Liz looked at the phone, still unsure if she was happy or sad that Matt probably wasn't the creep handing out rags and bloody glass. Of course, that left Rob as the most likely suspect as far as she was concerned. He was nearly as obnoxious as Matt, and she presumed he probably had the same bent moral compass. Liz opened the drawer and took one last look at the fabric scrap inside before heading to her room for the night. In the morning, she would make the time to track down the source of the blue wrapping paper and investigate the reporter more thoroughly.

Unfortunately, her plan for the morning involved getting a good night's sleep first, and that was wishful thinking. Within a few hours of crawling under the covers, the sound of barking jerked Liz from a deep sleep. Panic bloomed in her stomach as she jumped out of bed. Beans was not a dog prone to wakefulness or paranoia. If he was barking in the middle of the night, something must be wrong.

Liz wrapped a robe around herself as she hurried to the kitchen. The foyer felt icy-cold and drafty. Liz followed the chill to the utility room, where she found the side door standing wide open and Beans out on the stoop barking into the darkness. She stepped out to stand beside the stout dog. Beans quieted and looked up at her, his mouth hanging open in a proud, drool-dripping grin while his stubby tail wagged his whole hindquarters.

"Don't look at me that way," Liz said. "What were you barking at?" She held her robe close around her, shivering in the frosty night. The back floodlight revealed nothing out of the ordinary. Beans seemed to have lost interest in sounding the alert, so she hauled him back inside.

Liz had barely closed the side door before Mr. Shelton peeked in from the kitchen hallway. "I heard the dog barking," he said. "Is everything all right?"

Liz smiled reassuringly. "Yes, it's fine. Apparently the wind blew the back door open, and it scared Beans. I must not have closed the door as tightly as I thought before I locked it."

"I know how that can be." He eyed the door as he spoke. "We have an old house, and I've had the same thing happen. Minus the bulldog barking, though. At least having a furry alarm system means you're not trying to heat the outdoors while you sleep."

"Yes, but I'm sorry that Beans woke you. I know Mrs. Shelton needs her rest."

"It's all right. She takes a pill at bedtime, and she slept right through the barking. I'm a light sleeper, especially since Judy got sick."

"I can imagine."

Mr. Shelton bobbed his head. "Well, good night. I'll see you in the morning."

Liz turned back to the door, locking it firmly. Then when she pulled the knob to make certain the lock caught, the door pulled open again. "What is wrong with this thing?" She bent over to inspect the lock mechanism. It looked fine. Then as she pushed the door closed, she caught sight of a flash of white.

Liz knelt and examined the strike plate in the doorframe. Something had been wedged in the well where the door latch should have fit, keeping the lock from fully engaging. She dug out the tiny scrap and found it was simply a bit of wadded-up paper napkin.

Liz closed the door, firmly locking it, and glanced around the utility room. Nothing looked disturbed, but clearly someone had planned to come in the side door after it was locked.

But did they?

17

Over a breakfast of fluffy omelets and fruit, a tired Liz apologized to the guests for the commotion in the night. She'd stayed up for over an hour after locking the side door, double-checking window latches, and searching the inn in vain for signs of an intruder. Thankfully Beans had been a silent companion after his initial barking. The twin sisters claimed they hadn't heard anything.

"Must have been exciting for your dog," Gina said. "I know my chihuahua loved to go out at night and bark at all the smells."

"That dog just wanted to make noise," her sister grumbled, "all the time."

Gina glanced sidelong at her sister. "At least he didn't get fur on everything like some cats I could mention."

Before the griping could escalate, Vivian cut in. "I heard Beans bark, but I didn't think much of it and went back to sleep. It certainly wasn't disturbing."

"I never heard a thing," Arthur said. "I imagine that's one of the benefits of being on the third floor. Plus, I'm a heavy sleeper."

"I'm so glad none of you were bothered." Liz looked around at the guests and thought of how much nicer breakfast was without Matt and his new fiancée at the table. She could imagine the earful of complaints she would have gotten from those two about Beans's late-night barking.

"I'm a little sorry we missed all the action," Lois said before popping a hunk of melon into her mouth.

"It wasn't much action," Liz said. "Just the wind."

After breakfast, Liz cleared the table. Sarah helped her load the dishwasher and disappeared to clean the rooms Matt and Portia had vacated. Liz was putting on a fresh pot of coffee when both Sadie and Mary Ann entered the kitchen.

"We heard about your nighttime commotion. Are you sure it was only the wind?" Sadie asked as soon as the kitchen door swung closed.

"I certainly didn't see anyone," Liz said. "And Beans stopped barking right away, so whatever it was didn't particularly scare him. But it wasn't entirely the wind either." She explained about the paper napkin used to keep the lock from catching.

"Do you think that might have been Matt?" Mary Ann asked. "I don't want to accuse anyone falsely, but it sounds as if he wanted to come and go as he pleased while he was here. He might have rigged the door days ago and it took this long for the wind to blow it open."

Liz hated to think that she'd slept with the door only appearing to be locked for a couple of nights, but she had to admit it sounded reasonable. "Matt is the gift that keeps on giving."

Mary Ann poured a cup of coffee. "I assume you looked around to make sure nothing was taken?"

"The kitchen didn't look at all disturbed. I suspect that if there was someone, Beans didn't give the person time to take anything."

Sadie leaned against the counter. "So what's your plan for today?"

"I'm going to track down the source of the wrapping paper," Liz said as she wiped off the counters. "And I want to learn a little more about that newspaper reporter."

Sadie gave her a teasing grin. "Which one? Rob or the one you used to date?"

Liz rolled her eyes. "I don't think Matt is involved. I'd love for him to be the bad guy because it would make the whole thing less scary, but I don't think he is."

"Do you want me to go with you to track down the paper?" Mary Ann asked. "Since Sadie took a shop break yesterday, I could sneak away today."

"Wouldn't you rather do something with your cousin?" Liz poured herself another cup of coffee, hoping to chase away the fog clouding her sleepy brain.

Mary Ann peered at Liz over her own mug. "Arthur's heading upstate for the day to visit family on his mother's side, and the rest of my houseguests decided to go Christmas shopping. Since my shopping is done, I'm all yours if you want me."

"I'd love the company."

They heard a knock at the side door. Liz trotted through the hall to the utility room.

Jackson greeted her with his kind smile. "Good morning. May I come in?"

"Of course," Liz said warmly. She led him to the kitchen and offered him a cup of coffee.

As soon as she saw Jackson, Mary Ann spoke up. "Did you ask the chief about borrowing the scrap of cloth for me to look at?"

"Sorry, no evidence released to civilians," Jackson said. "Not even if they're the mayor."

"Oh!" Liz yelped. "I completely forgot." She hurried to the drawer . . . and froze. The bag she distinctly remembered putting in the drawer wasn't there. "It's gone!"

"What's gone?"

"I had a scrap of that flannel." Liz quickly brought the others up to speed on Beans's find. "And I put the baggie with the fabric in it right here. But it's gone."

Sadie walked over. "Maybe you put it in a different drawer." She began pulling open other drawers. After a quick search, it was obvious that the cloth was missing.

"I guess there really was an intruder last night," Mary Ann said fretfully.

"I can't believe Beans didn't scare the person off before he or she took it. That dog was making all kinds of racket when I woke up. How did someone manage to go through the drawers while being barked at like that?"

Jackson raised his hand, interrupting Liz's speculation. "What are you talking about? What intruder? Did you call the police?"

"I wasn't sure there *was* an intruder until just now," Liz said. "Beans woke me last night with his barking. When I came out to the kitchen, the back door was open and Beans was barking at the dark. I never saw anyone, and the dog didn't seem all that upset. There was no growling like he did at Matt. It was more like the sound he makes when he sees a squirrel. I really didn't think there had been an intruder."

"Tell Jackson what you found in the door lock." Sadie gave her a light nudge, but jumped in to tell him herself before Liz could speak. "Someone tampered with the lock."

Jackson's face darkened. "Tampered how?"

Liz explained about the bit of napkin she'd found stuffed in the lock. "Since I don't know when the person messed with the lock, I don't know if the wind blew open the door."

"I thought it was probably her ex," Sadie said. "We don't like him at all."

"Neither do I," Jackson said and looked at Liz. "What do you think? Did Matt break in here last night?"

Liz shook her head. "You saw Beans around Matt. There's no way that dog would have let him in without a lot of growling and maybe more. Besides, I talked to Matt on the phone. He said he flew back to Boston."

Jackson frowned. "He could say anything. That doesn't make it true."

"Matt could have brought the dog a treat," Mary Ann said. "I don't want to be disloyal to Beans, but his affections are rather easily bought with food."

Liz groaned and held her head. "So even when I think I'm sure of something, there are still questions."

"You say Beans was barking at the intruder outside?" Jackson asked.
Liz nodded. "That's what woke me up."

"I'm going to go out and look around. I'll take Beans with me.
Who knows? He might show me something." Jackson headed out
the door with the dog on his heels.

"I think he might be confusing that bulldog with Lassie," Sadie
said as she topped off her coffee.

Liz reached for her own mug, but stopped. If she drank any
more coffee she'd start shaking. "Beans is more like a beanbag chair
than a tracking hound."

"I have to go open the shop," Sadie said. "Good luck in your
hunt for the source of the wrapping paper."

While Mary Ann hung up a dish towel, Liz walked to her
quarters to grab her purse. She checked inside to make sure the
scrap of blue paper was still there and gave a small sigh of relief
when she saw that it was right where she'd left it.

When Liz got back to the kitchen, she found Jackson standing
in the middle of the room, a look of triumph on his face. He held
up a plastic bag with a small piece of cloth inside. "Look what I
found!"

Liz whooped. "Fantastic. Where?"

"It was caught in the bush, right outside the door. You said Beans
barked at the person outside? Maybe the dog scared the intruder
into dropping the bag. Then in the dark, he couldn't find it again."

"Maybe," Liz said.

Mary Ann took the bag from Jackson. She turned it over in her
hands, carefully inspecting the fabric's weave and pattern. "How
closely have you looked at this?"

"Not at all," Liz answered. "I noticed it was flannel, but that's
about it." She looked at Jackson. "Have you seen all the samples?
Does this match them?"

"It looks the same to me," Jackson said. "And the chief told me all the fabric they've collected comes from the same source."

"It's definitely flannel." Mary Ann slipped the piece from the bag. "But more specifically, it's flannel from some kind of child's clothing. My guess would be pajamas or a blanket. Look at this faded pattern in the light."

Liz stepped closer to peer at the faint blotches of color dulled by the gray of mold. "I can't tell what that is."

"I think it's a spaceship." Mary Ann traced the outline of the shape with her finger. "And I'm pretty sure this is a crescent moon. So this is definitely cloth from some kind of children's clothing or blanket."

Jackson took the fabric from her and peered at it. "That makes sense. It's the third thing we've seen that ties the boxes to a child." He ticked the items off on his fingers. "Baby teeth, a teddy bear's head, and these scraps of flannel cloth—somehow all this is related to a kid."

"Maybe someone lost a child," Mary Ann said, her face full of sympathy. "That would put an incredible strain on a person."

"Could be," Liz said. "Though, where would 'heartless' come in? Are the packages about someone who lost a child and didn't seem to care? Maybe the sender is suggesting that person is heartless."

Jackson shook his head. "But why leave them all over town? I've never lost a child, and I got one of these packages."

"It's all so confusing." Liz's voice was edged with frustration.

"I think we need to stick with investigating our suspects," Jackson said. "And if we assume Matt really is out of town, what suspects do we have left?"

"I really wonder about Rob." Liz thought back to the reporter's visit the night before. "He is definitely milking this for all the headlines he can. Plus, he's a reporter, so he might know some old story that he's resurrecting for his own benefit."

"I've never liked Rob much," Jackson admitted. "And I can see him exploiting a scoop for all it's worth once the story comes along. But I'm not sure I can picture him manufacturing one."

"It is a stretch," Liz said. "But Beans found a piece of cloth, and that means he came into contact with the person packing these things."

"Maybe," Jackson said.

"Probably," Liz insisted. "The more I think about it, the surer I am. Beans sat on Rob's foot repeatedly. Then he drove the guy away with one of his slobber baths. But what if Beans already had the fabric scrap in his mouth? Perhaps that's what made him drool."

"To be fair," Mary Ann said, "I think being an English bulldog is what made him drool." She caught a glimpse of Liz's face and quickly added, "But you could be right. Certainly it sounds like Beans was close enough to the reporter to get the cloth if Rob had it on him."

"I'm willing to consider the possibility," Jackson conceded. "I'd like to go over to Rob's office and talk to him."

"Sounds good. We'll come too," Liz said. "But Mary Ann and I are going to check out some shops first and see if we can find the source of the wrapping paper. That might be more productive than confronting Rob, though I would like to do both today."

"No problem. You and Mary Ann can do your paper search this morning. That will give me a chance to stop by my office and check on the business. This time of year, I don't want to make my manager handle everything."

"So we could meet around lunchtime," Liz suggested, "and go have a chat with Mr. Carver then."

Jackson agreed and they parted company. Liz grabbed a coat and scarf, and followed Mary Ann to the fabric shop.

"Should I make a list of places to visit?" Liz asked. "I could check the phone book."

"I know the shops that would be likely to have the wrapping

paper." Mary Ann pulled on her own coat. "The first is a short walk from here."

Liz gave her friend a one-armed hug. "It's good to work with a native."

"That's me."

When they left the inn, Liz was glad of her warm wool coat, corduroy slacks, and thick scarf. The morning air was cold and sharp, making her instinctively hunch her shoulders in defense as she walked down the street with Mary Ann beside her.

As was often the case, Pleasant Creek's charm helped lift Liz's spirits as they walked. In place of the usual hanging plants, wreaths decorated the old-fashioned gas lamps that lined the downtown streets. Every person they passed offered a smile, and many spoke a greeting. Of course, it didn't hurt that Mary Ann responded to most by name.

"Do you know everyone?" Liz asked her after about a dozen such interactions.

Mary Ann laughed. "I think I'm simply good with names, but I did grow up here. Plus, between the shop, various fundraisers, and church, I have met most of Pleasant Creek's population."

"I could walk around in Boston all day and not meet anyone I knew by name. Not that Bostonians aren't good people, but there are just so many."

"Pleasant Creek can get a little crowded in the summer," Mary Ann said. "And then I definitely won't know the name of everyone we pass. But I think Indiana winters scare away most of the tourists."

"Thankfully not all of them, or the inn would be in trouble." Liz shivered and pulled her scarf closer around her neck. She looked up at the sky. "It looks a little like snow."

Mary Ann turned her face up as well. "That would be nice. I love a white Christmas. As long as we don't get so snowed in that Arthur can't make his flight home on the day after." She pointed ahead of them. "This is the first shop that might have the paper."

Though the shop was charming and Liz bought some beautiful hand-painted note cards while they were there, the owner didn't recognize the scrap of paper that Liz showed him. The women walked several blocks to the next store and received nearly the same response.

"I've never carried anything like that," the silver-haired owner said, tapping the scrap. "I have seen it, though."

Liz's eyes widened. "Where?"

"On one of those disgusting packages that have been turning up around town. We got one this morning. I had my husband drop it by the police station." She shuddered. "Why would someone do something so foul at Christmas?"

"That's what I want to know," Liz said.

"Good luck with it."

Mary Ann and Liz chatted with proprietors of two more places—a gift shop and a print shop. Neither had seen the paper or gotten a package. "I hope it stays that way," the print-shop owner said before he knocked on his old wooden counter for luck.

The ladies stepped out of the cozy print shop and immediately huddled closer. The weather was definitely not warming as the morning progressed.

"I only know of one other possibility," Mary Ann said. "It's a couple of blocks that way." She pointed off to the right. "It's another print shop, though it doesn't do a lot of business. The owner is getting older and basically opens only when he feels like it."

"So we might walk over there and find the shop closed." Liz thought for a moment. "Maybe we should call ahead."

"We can try, but another of Mr. Gately's quirks is that he answers the phone only if it suits him."

Liz stared at her friend. "How does he stay in business?"

Mary Ann shrugged. "He owns the building and several others

in town. He doesn't have any family, and I don't think he needs the money. He only opens the shop when he's bored."

"Well, let's hope he's bored today. I don't want to leave any stone unturned," Liz said, walking swiftly to help stay warm. The shop was tucked between a shoe-repair store and an appliance-repair shop. "This seems to be the street time forgot. I can't remember the last time I saw a shoe-repair store."

"It's owned by an Amish couple." Mary Ann waved through the cobbler's window at the folks inside. "They're darling, and they run the whole business with no electricity. The Amish are a little less likely to discard something when it starts to get worn, so businesses like this are able to survive, barely, in Pleasant Creek." Then she turned to Liz with a grin. "This is where Sadie got her cowboy boots resoled."

"Cowboy boots?" Liz echoed. "Sadie Schwarzentruber owns cowboy boots?"

"Handmade in Texas."

Liz shook her head. "She never ceases to surprise."

The print shop had no sign indicating whether it was opened or closed, and the window over the door was in need of a good cleaning. Liz turned the knob and the door swung inward. A blast of heat struck her in the face, like opening the oven door at the inn. Initially it was welcoming, but Liz suspected she would quickly grow too warm in the shop.

She saw a teenage girl seated on a stool behind the counter, poking at her cell phone screen and chewing a sizable piece of gum. The girl looked up at them and offered a bright smile. "How can I help you?"

"Where's Mr. Gately?" Mary Ann asked, clearly startled to see a girl instead of an elderly man.

"On vacation," the teen said. "Florida. Can you believe it? Who would go to Florida for Christmas?"

Liz pulled the scrap of paper from her pocket and held it out. "Have you ever seen paper like this?"

"I should hope so," the girl said. "Mr. Gately made it."

18

Feeling a rush of excitement, Liz exchanged glances with Mary Ann. They'd made their first connection to a solid breakthrough.

"I don't suppose you have a list of people who have bought this wrapping paper?" Liz asked.

The teenager shook her head, sending her ponytail swinging. "I haven't sold any of it." She rolled her eyes. "I haven't sold much of anything. We're not exactly on the beaten path here, and the people who do come in seem to be surprised the shop is open. It's weird."

"How long have you been working here?" Liz's bubble of optimism was threatening to burst.

"All this week. Mr. Gately is sort of my great-uncle. I mean, he's not related to me really, but he was best friends with my grandpa, so my dad grew up calling him an uncle." She grinned. "Anyway, all that means is that when he wanted to go to Florida, he gave me the job of looking after this place, which is good because he paid me in advance and that meant I could buy Christmas presents this year."

"That was nice of him," Liz said. "I don't suppose Mr. Gately kept a record of people who bought that paper."

The girl shook her head. "I did see him sell some last week when I came by for my training, which was extremely boring."

"Last week?" Liz's hope swelled again. "Do you know which day?"

The girl gave Liz look that suggested she worried about Liz's mental acuity. "Of course, it was my training day." In response to Liz raising her eyebrows in a questioning look, the girl added, "Friday."

Mary Ann must have sensed Liz's frustration, because she stepped in with a smile before Liz could say anything too snippy to the young clerk. "Do you have access to the receipts from Friday?"

The girl snapped her gum and nodded. "I have to, in case someone wants to return something or complain. Not that anyone has. Mr. Gately does good work."

"I'm sure he does," Mary Ann said sweetly. "Could you check to see who bought the paper? If the person paid with a credit card, you should have a name."

"Right." The girl slid off the stool and walked over to a file drawer. She pulled out a folder and flipped through a couple slips of paper. "I found it. The sale was cash. No name." She held up the slip so Liz and Mary Ann could see it.

Liz sighed with disappointment. "Do you remember anything at all about the buyer?"

"I didn't pay much attention. It was just paper, you know. I only remember because Mr. Gately is super proud of that paper. It's, like, his favorite stuff." The girl paused, thinking. "The buyer was a man, and not really old. I mean, too old for me to date him, but not all gray and wrinkly."

"Do you remember if he was tall or short?" Liz asked. "You said his hair wasn't gray. Was it blond? Black?"

"I don't know. I didn't wait on him. It was a man. He bought paper. That's it."

"Do you suppose you could call Mr. Gately and see if he remembers anything more?" Liz's pulse raced. "It's pretty important. This paper has been connected to a crime."

The girl gave Liz a doubtful look. "A wrapping paper crime?"

"Can you please just call Mr. Gately and ask him about this?" Liz's impatience threatened to resurface.

"Nope. I mean, I would, since you say it's important, but he didn't leave me a number."

"How would you contact him if there was an emergency?" Mary Ann asked.

The girl shrugged. "He said if there was an emergency, he didn't want to know. He said he hadn't taken a real vacation in thirty years, and he didn't care if the whole store burned down while he was gone. He'd sort it out when he got back."

Lacking anything else to ask, Liz and Mary Ann finally thanked the girl for her time and left the shop. They'd barely gotten out to the sidewalk when Liz's phone rang. She fished it out of her coat pocket and focused on talking without her teeth chattering in the cold. "Hello?"

"Hi, Liz," Jackson said. "How goes the paper hunt?"

"We found the shop, but it hasn't helped much." As she and Mary Ann began the long walk back to the inn, Liz described their encounter with the young print-shop clerk.

"Wow, I can't believe Mr. Gately went on a vacation." Jackson sounded genuinely surprised. "He doesn't seem the Christmas-in-Florida type."

"There's a type for that?" Liz asked.

"Maybe. And if there is, Mr. Gately seems like he wouldn't be a match. If you're done with the paper search, I can meet you to talk with Rob Carver. The newspaper office isn't too far from Mr. Gately's shop."

"Great, do you want me to come over there?"

"Sounds good. After we talk to Rob, I'll take you two ladies out to lunch."

Liz passed the invitation on to Mary Ann, but she shook her head. "Thank him for me, but I need to get back to Sew Welcome." Then she tapped Liz on the arm. "Don't forget the cookie swap with the Material Girls is this afternoon."

Liz's eyes widened. "I had completely forgotten." She began to calculate her schedule in her head. She should have time to meet with the reporter and then get back to the inn and make her nutty fudge bars. "I'll be there."

Mary Ann smiled. "Well, if Jackson whisks you off somewhere and you miss the swap, I expect you'll be forgiven. Though I warn you, Sadie will tease you terribly."

"I'm sure."

They reached a cross street, and Mary Ann turned toward the inn. Liz went in the other direction to reach the newspaper office, which she'd been to a couple of times to discuss advertising for the inn when she'd first bought it. Ultimately, though, promotions online and in country magazines had yielded better exposure than the local paper.

Liz reached the office as Jackson pulled up in the well-maintained older pickup that he drove for work. He parked in front of the building and waved at Liz as she walked over.

"You got here quick," he said as he climbed out of the truck.

"In this cold, it doesn't pay to dawdle." Liz fervently hoped the chilly air hadn't turned her nose red.

They walked together to the front door of the newspaper, only to find it locked.

Liz leaned close to peer through the glass. "I don't see anyone moving around in there."

"It's noon. I forgot they close for lunch." Jackson pointed across the street to a small sandwich shop. "As I remember, most of the staff eats there, so we may be able to grab some food and ask Rob questions at the same time. You'll love the place. It's run by a brother and sister from New York. The food isn't exactly low-calorie, but it is delicious."

"Sounds good." The thought of a hot beverage alone was enough to make Liz pick up the pace as they crossed the street.

The sandwich shop was long and narrow with a glass-front counter displaying meats and cheeses, much like a grocery deli. A chalkboard stretching along the wall behind the counter listed their menu and prices, as well as the artisan sodas available.

A stocky, broad-shouldered man in a white apron gave them a welcoming grin. "Mr. Mayor. Nice to see you out this way."

"Thanks, Sid." Jackson introduced Liz as he gave a cursory glance at the mostly filled booths that lined the walls. "Is Rob Carver here?"

Sid shook his head. "He's usually in about this time, but not today. Can I get you two some lunch?"

Jackson glanced at Liz, who nodded. When they placed their order, Liz chose hot coffee over the locally bottled soda.

Sid leaned close to the counter to mutter a warning to Liz. "You might want the soda. My sister made the coffee this morning, and it's a little strong."

"I like it strong. And I'm hoping a hot beverage will help me feel my fingers again." At the mention of the cold, Liz rubbed her hands together in front of her instinctively.

"I hear ya," Sid said, pouring her a mug of coffee.

Jackson led her to a booth, and they settled in. Liz took a sip of the coffee and wrinkled her nose.

"Strong?" Jackson asked.

Liz swallowed the bitter brew and nodded as she reached for sweetener. "But it's hot. And I was warned."

Jackson turned his gaze again to the other booths. "I see a couple of people from the paper here. Maybe Rob will come in before we're done."

"I don't mind a chance to sit down inside. Traipsing around Pleasant Creek in the cold was both picturesque and frigid."

Jackson sipped the birch root beer he'd chosen. "It's too bad Mr. Gately took his vacation without leaving a phone number."

"It's weird. Who leaves their business in the hands of a teenager and doesn't give her a number to call in case of emergency?"

"Mr. Gately has always been quirky."

"Mary Ann did mention his casual approach to business hours," Liz said. Then, she had a thought that made her frown. "You said he's quirky. Is he quirky enough to leave creepy packages all over town?"

"That would be a little hard for him to do from Florida, don't you think?" Jackson asked.

"We only know that he *said* he was going to Florida. And he left no number. What if that's because there isn't a Florida number? What if he's still here, leaving mystery gifts wrapped in the paper he made himself?"

"That's an interesting theory. But why would he leave those packages?"

Liz shrugged. "Why would anyone? Maybe he's upset about his business being slow? Or he's upset about being all alone? Maybe he thinks it's because the whole town is heartless?"

Jackson looked doubtful. "Mr. Gately has never struck me as bitter. A little odd, yes, but not angry or vindictive."

The conversation was interrupted by an appearance from Sid, delivering their lunches. Liz bit into her thick sandwich and made a sound of delight at the burst of flavors.

"I told you that you'd love it," Jackson said with a grin.

Conversation simply had to wait until they were both finished. When she was full, Liz looked down at her mostly empty basket; a few of the homemade chips and half a pickle reminded her that she could never be called a picky eater. "I love this place. I must forget all about it before I swell up like a balloon. How can the newspaper staff eat here all the time?"

"I guess chasing stories burns calories," Jackson said. Suddenly he tapped the back of Liz's hand and subtly jerked his head toward a booth where two people were gathering their lunch trash and getting up. "They work for the paper."

"So we follow them back to the office?"

"That's the plan."

With a full stomach, Liz felt the icy chill wasn't able to cut through her as deeply when she stepped outside, but it still made her grit her teeth at first. She wondered if the temperature had actually dropped since morning. Even Jackson hunched his broad shoulders against the cold and crammed his hands in the pockets of the thick leather jacket he wore.

By the time they'd crossed the street, the two reporters from the paper were already inside the building. Liz was grateful when the door opened easily as soon as they reached it. The newspaper office was cooler than the diner had been, but still a welcome relief from the sharp winter air.

One of the two people they'd followed, a woman whose dark hair was liberally sprinkled with gray, looked up at them from her desk. "May I help you?" She squinted, picked up a pair of glasses, slipped them on, and smiled. "Jackson, what a surprise."

He nodded in greeting. "Hi, Marty. We're looking for Rob Carver. Have you seen him?"

"He was here earlier. But he left before lunch."

The other reporter, standing next to a big scanner, turned to join the conversation. "Yeah. He was a bear all morning, hunched over his computer. Then he yells, 'Eureka!' and practically runs out of here after seeing something on his screen." He shrugged. "We figured he'd found Bigfoot or some other nutty lead."

"Now, Oliver." Marty gave the man a disapproving look, but seemed to reconsider. "Well, Rob does enjoy chasing unusual stories."

"You mean sensational stories," Liz said. "I've noticed. He has my guests at the Olde Mansion Inn scared half to death with his article about the packages."

"Yeah, that's a good example," Oliver said. "Only Rob would turn some kid's creepy prank into the crime of the century."

"Do you think whatever he discovered might have been related to those packages?" Jackson asked, looking around the newsroom. "Which desk is his?"

"Now, now." Marty had a note of scolding in her voice. "We can't let you poke around Rob's computer."

"I wouldn't dream of it." Jackson held up his hands innocently. "I want to leave him a note."

Marty gave him a doubtful expression, but she pointed across the room. Located under a flickering fluorescent light in the corner, Rob's desk assignment clearly wasn't optimal. No wonder the reporter was desperate to advance or escape.

Liz followed Jackson to the desk, where the mayor picked up a pad of paper and bent over it with a pen. Marty watched them for a moment, but her phone rang and pulled her attention away. While she wasn't looking, Jackson bumped the mouse on Rob's desk and his computer screen lit up.

The image on the screen showed a scan of an old newspaper article. Liz leaned closer to make out the grainy black-and-white image of a car crumpled against a tree. From the snow on the car, it was obviously winter. "Do you suppose that's the accident that produced those shards of glass?"

"It seems as though Rob thought so." Jackson leaned closer to the screen as well.

The scan of the article wasn't the highest resolution, so making out the newspaper print was challenging. But Jackson and Liz were able to decipher that the car had slid on an icy road on Christmas Eve and slammed head-on into a tree. A man and his wife had been removed from the wreck and declared dead at the scene.

"How horrible," Liz whispered.

"Why would this accident in particular interest a reporter?" Jackson's tone suggested he was asking himself as much as Liz. "Why would he think it's tied to the packages?"

"It does seem like a loose connection," Liz said. "Wouldn't you expect a mention of a child? The contents of those packages point to a child even more than to an accident."

At the sound of throat clearing, they both looked up from the computer screen to find Marty with her arms crossed, standing in front of the desk and frowning down at them. "You don't look like you're writing a note."

Jackson pointed at the screen. "This could be important. Do you have Rob's cell phone number? I have some questions for him."

Marty's frown lingered for another moment, but she squinted at the screen, skimming the information there. With a sigh, she lifted a pile of papers spread over one side of the reporter's desk to reveal a business-card holder. "His cell number is on his card."

"Thanks." Jackson snatched up a card and backed away from the computer to appease Marty.

She followed him around the desk and watched him sharply as he dialed.

After a few moments, Jackson held up the phone so they could hear the result. The call had simply rolled to voice mail. Jackson left a brief message requesting a call back. "So he missed lunch and now he's not answering his phone." Jackson looked at Marty. "Doesn't that make you wonder?"

"Honestly, Jackson," she said. "Everything about that man makes me wonder."

19

While Jackson distracted Marty, Liz turned back to the computer, clicking through the other browser windows Rob had left open. She froze when she found photos of the couple killed in the crash. Something about them seemed familiar. "Jackson, look at this."

"I told you two to leave that alone," Marty said, but she followed Jackson back to the computer and peered at the screen along with him.

The photos on the screen came from the couple's driver's licenses, and they weren't very clear. Still, that feeling that she'd seen them before lingered. "Do you know them?" Liz asked.

Jackson leaned close and studied the images. He shrugged. "I don't think I ever met them." He pointed at the information below the photos. "They weren't from Pleasant Creek. That area is south of here."

Liz turned to Marty. "Any chance you remember this accident?"

Marty shook her head. "It's a sad story, dying on Christmas Eve, so I'm sure I would have read it at the time. I don't remember it, though." She smiled. "I still had kids at home back then. That was before my newspaper career."

Before Liz could question Marty further, Jackson's cell phone rang. "Is it Rob?" Liz asked.

The mayor shook his head as he spoke into the phone. "Chief Houghton, what can I do for you?"

Liz fidgeted while Jackson replied with a series of uninformative grunts to whatever the police chief said. She noticed that Marty's attention had sharpened as well, and she hoped Jackson would be careful about whatever he said. They weren't exactly in the right place for sensitive information to be discussed.

Finally, Jackson ended the call and smiled at Liz. "Well, we should be going."

"Whoa," Marty said. "Aren't you going to let us know what's going on, Mayor? Your constituents need to know."

Jackson addressed the newspaperwoman without flinching. "Not this time, Marty. But you can let Rob know I'm looking for him when you see him." He herded Liz out of the office while Marty continued to call out complaints about the public's right to be informed.

Once they were outside, Jackson turned to Liz while keeping a sharp eye on the newspaper office door. "There's been another package delivery," he said quietly. "Thankfully, this one didn't come with an unconscious citizen. I'm going over to check it out. You can come, or I can drop you back by the inn."

As much as the warm inn sounded appealing, Liz's curiosity was working overtime, especially with the nagging feeling that she'd seen the accident victims before. "I don't need to be back for a while."

Jackson's face lit up. "Great. Let's go."

Along the way, Jackson explained that the package had appeared outside a small store on the very edge of town. "The shop belongs to a Mennonite couple. They sell Amish cheese and preserves from the local community to people passing by on their way to bigger cities."

"So whoever is leaving the packages is no longer sticking to downtown businesses and the buggies that stop in town."

"Apparently not." Jackson frowned. "I don't like the feeling of escalation. It's slow escalation, but we're seeing uglier contents, and now the recipients are getting more spread out as well." He shook his head. "It makes me wonder where this guy is planning to go with this."

"So you think it's a man?" Liz asked.

"Mrs. Henderson seemed to believe it was a man."

"Well, she was sure it was a tall person. But I've met some very tall women, including Portia."

Jackson offered her a sideways smile. "You can actually picture your ex's new fiancée handling dead mice and blood-spattered glass?"

"When you put it that way, I suppose not."

When they reached the cheese shop, Liz was struck by how different it looked from the quaint businesses in downtown Pleasant Creek. Instead, the building was basically a stark white box that sat alone on the road. Surrounded by low-growing brush and sparse trees on two sides, the shop had no windows beyond the two that faced the parking lot.

More than half full of cars, the parking lot was worn pavement spotted with patched potholes. Liz hopped down from the truck before Jackson could rush around and open the door for her. She appreciated the chivalry, but she was eager to find out what was going on. She led the way for a moment, but was soon trotting along in Jackson's long-legged wake as he headed over to the knot of police officers in front of the building.

Officer Hughes caught sight of them approaching and nodded toward the door. "The chief's inside."

"Thanks," Jackson said, holding the door open for Liz.

The young Mennonite couple who owned the shop stood by the front counter, talking to the chief. The woman wore a dark dress with a thick wool sweater and a sheer white prayer cap. She offered Liz a polite bob of the head and shy smile as Jackson introduced them. The husband wore dark slacks, a blue work shirt, and a canvas jacket. He lacked the beard Liz normally saw on the Amish men of his age, but his serious expression wasn't much different.

Jackson asked what they'd found in the box.

"More rags," Chief Houghton said. "And a cat."

"A kitten, really." The Mennonite woman's voice was soft but serious. "Just a wee thing."

Liz's eyes widened in horror. "This guy killed a kitten?"

"Oh, no," she said quickly. "The kitten is alive. It's in a carton behind the counter, nice and warm."

The chief acknowledged the woman's words with a nod. "A live kitten. It's very young, though. If the Fishers hadn't found the package as quickly as they did, the little thing would have died in this cold."

"It was crying." Mrs. Fisher's eyes widened as she recounted her discovery. "I don't think it should be away from its mother so soon. It's a good thing we have goat's milk in the shop. I warmed some and fed the kitten. I think it will be all right."

"We have to assume that whoever left the box didn't care if the kitten lived or died," the chief said.

"Maybe that was the point," Liz suggested. "That somehow whether the kitten lived or died depended on the people who found the package. Maybe that's tied to the *Heartless* cards somehow."

"Heartless," Mr. Fisher said with a snort. "That is what a person must be to leave a tiny kitten out in the cold. I couldn't have done it."

Neither could I. As Liz thought about shoving a tiny kitten in a box and leaving it out in the freezing weather, she shivered, wrapping her arms around herself. Her gaze swept over the store as the police chief spoke of efforts to put a stop to the sinister packages. She wondered if Rob was going to show up and use this box to further frighten the people of Pleasant Creek.

Liz looked out the front window, expecting to see the reporter storming up to the door. Instead, she saw that the parking lot hosted a small audience of people sitting at their steering wheels or standing just outside their cars, looking toward the store and the gathering of police cars. She exchanged gazes with the person closest, a woman who huddled at the front bumper of a station wagon and stared though the shop window. The woman looked more than cold. She looked scared. *This isn't what Christmas is supposed to be.*

Then Liz was surprised to realize she recognized one of the people standing beside a car. At the back of the group, Charlie stood leaning against a battered gray Volkswagen van at the far end of the parking lot, his arms crossed over his chest.

"I'll be right back," Liz said as she opened the shop door. With no real explanation as to what compelled her, Liz wove her way through the cars toward the van. She nodded at the frightened woman as she passed, but kept up a rapid pace to reach the storyteller. "Hi, Charlie," she said as she approached him. "Cold day to stand around outside, huh?"

"I was hoping to get some cheese," he said. "This is my favorite cheese shop. It's good and cheap at the same time, a rare combination." He nodded toward the policemen. "Do you know what they're here for?"

Liz nodded solemnly. "Another one of those troubling packages."

Charlie frowned. "That's still going on? The newspaper made the packages sound so terrible, but I thought they might be a prank or something."

"Or something." Liz looked back toward the policemen. "The police are only being careful. They want to keep the town safe. And the packages are ruining a lot of Christmases."

"We wouldn't want anyone's Christmas ruined around here," Charlie said, his voice suddenly sharp.

The storyteller's tone jerked Liz's gaze back to him. He gave her his amiable smile, but the remark about Christmas had sounded anything but friendly.

Liz blinked as a realization hit her. She knew why the couple in the accident photo looked familiar. The man had the same boyish looks as Charlie, but he was fair with freckles, while Charlie had the same thick dark hair as the woman. The two people from the car accident were related to Charlie. "Your parents?" she whispered.

"My parents?" His eyes narrowed.

Liz took a step back, but Charlie closed the distance between them in a moment, grabbing her by the arm. She yelped, but he shoved her through the side door of the van so quickly she didn't have time to scream. He climbed in behind her, pulling the door shut, and Liz scooted away from him and opened her mouth to yell as loudly as possible.

Charlie produced a knife, seemingly from nowhere, and the blade gleamed in the shadowy interior of the van. "I don't want to hurt you, but you have to come with me, and I would prefer it if you didn't yell."

"Charlie," she whispered. "Did you leave those boxes?"

"I had to." The charming, boyish storyteller was completely gone. In his place was someone darker, someone who was making it difficult for Liz to catch her breath through her fear. "I had to find out who was heartless. I had to make the right people pay."

"People like me?" Liz asked softly.

Charlie shook his head. "I don't think you're one of them. But that doesn't mean I'll let you get in the way."

Liz's gaze flickered to the van's tinted windows. *Jackson, notice I'm missing.*

"We need to go."

"I'll scream."

"If you scream, I'll have to hurt you. And if you cause me any trouble, I can promise that Rob will have a horrible accident too. It's winter in Indiana. Fatal accidents happen all the time. But around here, they barely interrupt anyone's Christmas celebrations at all."

"I don't know what happened to your parents." Liz's voice trembled. "But what you're doing isn't right."

Charlie grunted and held out his hand. "Give me your cell phone."

Thinking fast, Liz pointed out through the front window. "It's in my purse in the mayor's truck."

Charlie shoved the knife into his belt and grabbed her arm again. He quickly went through her coat pockets, holding up the phone when he found it. "I know you only lied because you're scared, but I don't appreciate being lied to. You shouldn't do it again."

He climbed past her into the driver's seat. She lunged for the van's side door, only to realize there was no handle. The van had clearly been modified so a person could get in but not out.

"Buckle up," Charlie called over his shoulder.

"Can I ride in the front?" she asked as he cranked the engine. "I get carsick in the back." If he let her into the front seat, she could get out through that door or at least signal to Jackson or the chief.

"Not yet. I don't want anyone to see you." He turned once to smile at her, the boyish look back. "You don't need to be afraid. I don't want to hurt you."

Reluctantly, Liz buckled her seat belt and whispered a quiet prayer. If she couldn't get out of the van, maybe she could at least keep Charlie from doing whatever he had planned. "Do you know where Rob Carver is?"

Charlie's eyes met hers in the rearview mirror as the van roared to life. "Yes. You'll see him soon."

"Have you hurt him?"

Charlie frowned as they drove slowly out of the lot and onto the road. "No. You act like I'm some kind of monster. *I'm* the one who's suffered. I'm the one who should have been protected. Have you seen the garbage Rob writes for the newspaper?"

"I've read it."

"He's one of them."

"One of who?" Liz asked.

"One of the heartless ones. He loved those packages. He loved thinking about the dead things and the blood and the little kid. It was all a story to him."

"I thought you enjoyed stories. Isn't that what you do—tell stories?"

"I don't take the bad things in life and make them worse."

"Isn't that what the packages do?" Liz asked. "You give them to people who haven't done anything wrong. Doesn't that make things worse?"

Again, he frowned at her in the rearview mirror. "I had to do that. It's a test. I know it's a hard test, but I had to do it. That way I know which people to protect."

"Protect them from what?"

Charlie didn't answer. He wouldn't even look at her in the mirror. As they drove down the road, heading even farther from town, the question continued to ring in Liz's mind.

Protect them from what?

20

As soon as the van was out of sight of the cheese shop, but before they reached the first turn, Charlie rolled down the window and threw out Liz's cell phone. Liz morosely watched it sail into the roadside brush. She had a fleeting thought about how hard it would be to rebuild her contact list before she realized how ridiculous it was to worry about a contact list when she was riding in the back of a van driven by a very disturbed young man.

Desperate to keep Charlie talking, Liz said, "I assume it was you who rigged my door lock. Why did you want to be able to sneak into my inn?"

His glance darted to the rearview mirror again. "I planned to keep an eye on that guy who was staying there, the one who mocked my storytelling. I thought he was one of them, one of the heartless ones."

Can't argue with him on that, Liz thought. "You took the cloth from the drawer."

"I found it when I was looking for more information on your guests. I don't want to hurt *you,* but I'm not sure about all of them. Not yet."

Liz thought of the kind people staying at the inn and felt the knot of fear in her stomach tighten. She couldn't let this young man hurt them.

Charlie made turn after turn, taking them onto rougher and rougher roads until Liz was thoroughly lost. She gave up on her fantasy of the police pulling over the van and rescuing her, concentrating instead on not giving in to the urge to cry.

After the last turn onto a dirt road riddled with potholes and rocks, they bumped up to an old barn, clearly long abandoned. "It's a little cold in there," Charlie said. "But it felt appropriate. It reminds me of my childhood."

"Charlie, I don't know what happened to you, but . . ."

The storyteller hopped out of the van before Liz could finish her sentence. She quickly unbuckled her seat belt and turned sideways. She rocked back, bracing herself to kick out at Charlie as soon as she had a chance.

Charlie pulled open the van door and immediately ducked to one side as Liz's legs struck out. As her leg flashed past him, he grabbed her ankle and pulled, making her tumble out of the van.

"I'm trying hard not to get annoyed with you." Charlie grabbed her arm and hauled her to her feet, once again showing her the long knife he'd threatened her with in the parking lot. "But you're starting to make that difficult."

"You can't begin to guess how bad I feel for making things difficult for you." Sarcasm momentarily hid the fear in Liz's voice, and she struggled to free her arm from his grasp.

Charlie didn't respond. He simply hauled her toward the barn. The affable young man who'd told stories in her sitting room seemed to have vanished completely. Liz barely recognized the grim-faced villain who pulled open the barn door. As she was dragged along beside him, her eyes strayed again and again to the wicked blade in his hand.

Charlie closed the door behind them. The interior of the barn was shadowy, with little of the late afternoon light showing through the high, dusty windows. A battered old kerosene heater in the center of the barn offered some respite from the cold, but the temperature was still far from comfortable. Several barn cats milled around near the heater, clearly taking advantage of the unexpected warmth.

Not far from the heater, she spotted Rob seated on a crumbling bale of hay with his back against one of the barn supports. He was tied to the beam with rope and duct tape. As Liz and Charlie approached the heater, Rob raised his head to look at them. Liz saw bruises on his face and swelling around one eye.

"Are you all right?" Liz asked.

"Peachy." The reporter nearly spit out the word.

"Charlie, what are you doing?" Liz turned attention back to her captor. "What's this all about?"

The storyteller let go of her arm and smiled, giving Liz a glimpse of the young man she'd thought she knew. "As you and Mr. Carver here have figured out, my parents were in that car accident. We were driving home from an unsuccessful attempt to spend Christmas with my father's mother. She was an unpleasant woman who didn't seem to want me around, and she liked my mother even less." He sighed. "My mother didn't want me to have Christmas with such a person and insisted we go home, even if it meant driving through the night. She thought it was important that I wake up in my own bed on Christmas Day."

"She must have loved you," Liz said.

"Mothers do love their children, generally." Charlie gazed at the knife blade. "Don't they?"

"I believe so. I know I love my godson very much. His parents died in an accident too, when he was a little boy. After that he came to live with me."

Charlie looked at her, curiosity clear on his face. "Does he remember his parents?"

Liz nodded. "Though it's a mix, I suppose, of true memories and the stories I've told him about them."

"Stories are important," Charlie agreed. He pointed to another hay bale with the tip of the knife blade. "Sit, and I'll tell you the rest of my story."

Liz obeyed.

"The weather was awful that night, and my parents were mad

at each another so the car was quiet. I fell asleep. I know now that the car slid off the road and hit a tree. They may have hit a patch of ice. Or maybe my father nodded off, the same way I did. No one knows for certain."

"I'm so sorry." Liz rubbed her hands together to combat the chill she felt both physically and emotionally.

Charlie continued as if she hadn't spoken. "I woke up cold, in the dark, buckled up in the back of the car. My head hurt some, but I didn't know why. When I called to my mother, she didn't answer. I tried to open the door, but it was stuck, so I crawled out the window. It was so cold and I don't remember much, but I ended up in a barn." He gestured around. "It was a lot like this one, but not as run down."

"You must have been afraid."

"It's all a blur, really. I do know I was cold, but I burrowed into the hay, and the barn cats came and cuddled up with me. I fell asleep with only the purring cats, my flannel pajamas, and a ratty blanket I found in the barn to help keep me warm."

"Surely someone found you," Liz said.

He snorted. "By accident. No one was *looking* for me. Even after they found the car, even after they found my parents, they weren't *looking* for me."

"They would have if they'd known you were there."

"Do you truly believe that?" he asked. "Because I don't. The toys and the old teddy bear in the backseat should have been clues enough. How could they not know a little kid was lost in the cold and the snow after they found the car? No, they simply didn't care. No one in this *pleasant* little town cared."

"But someone *did* find you, or you wouldn't be here."

Charlie nodded. "The Amish farmer who owned the barn found me before sunrise. He carried me home to his family. They put warm clothes on me. They fed me and were kind."

"So not everyone was heartless, even in your memory." Liz recognized the similarities between this story and the one he'd told at the inn. "Why are you leaving packages in the buggies around town? The Amish weren't unkind to you."

"Weren't they?" He sneered. "They were worst of all, because they made me believe that I was safe. The wife wanted to keep me there through Christmas Day, but her husband said I was an English boy and an English problem. He put me in a cold buggy and drove me to town to hand me over to the kind police of Pleasant Creek."

His tone had turned so bitter that Liz was sure whatever came next in the story couldn't be good. She watched the young man pace back and forth in front of the heater for a moment, as though gathering his thoughts. His movements disturbed the barn cats, making them scramble back to the various bales of hay. One cat sauntered over and sniffed at Liz's boot.

"There wasn't an open foster home," he continued, "not at Christmas. So I was shoved into a group home. And the kids there were angry about their own problems. They didn't mind taking it out on the new kid. I spent a *year* in that home, until my dad's cousin found me and got me out of there."

"Well, boohoo," Rob sneered. "You had a tough time as a kid. Lots of people have tough childhoods, but they don't break the law."

Charlie whirled to face the other man so quickly it made Liz jump. "Shut up!" He threw his knife at Rob, and it buried itself deep in the wooden beam a few inches above the reporter's head.

Rob's face turned ashen.

With visible effort, Charlie calmed himself and spoke more quietly. "Of course you'd say that. You're just like them. Why should one little kid interrupt anyone's Christmas plans? Why should you have to face the kind of people you really are?"

"Charlie, you have to know that there are a lot of good people in Pleasant Creek," Liz said.

He laughed coldly. "A lot? No. Some, though. I believe there are some. That's what the packages are for, to help me find them."

"How do they help?" she asked.

"I listen." Charlie held his index finger to his ear for effect. "I listen to what people say about them. I listen for the ones who want to understand." He took a step closer to Liz, and it took a lot of effort for her not to shrink back. "I wouldn't have left you one if I'd known about you. I didn't know about your godson. About how you took him in when his parents died. You didn't let him rot in some group home. You seemed kind and now I know for sure—you're not one of them."

"Then you should let me go," Liz pleaded with her words and eyes.

Charlie went on as if he hadn't heard her. "I listen. So few people know how to listen, but that's what storytellers do. We listen, and we learn. I learned about this town—the bad parts and the good. I didn't want to do it wrong."

"Do what wrong?"

"The punishment."

Liz shuddered with a chill that had nothing to do with the cold in the barn. She folded her arms around her middle, hugging herself against the ice forming in her stomach. At that moment, a cat jumped up on the hay bale beside her and huddled against her side. She thought of the cats from Charlie's story and wondered what the horror of his childhood experience was driving him to do. "Punishment?" she finally echoed.

Charlie smiled, seeming pleased by her question. "It won't be too much," he assured her. "I'm not unfair. I simply plan to give them one bad Christmas. That's what they gave me. A bad Christmas that stretched into a bad year, a year that I never forgot. That's what I've got in store for this town."

"And you plan to do this by giving them worse and worse packages?"

He shook his head. "The packages were a test. I told you that. They aren't the punishment. That comes later."

"How much later?" Liz whispered.

"Tomorrow. Christmas Eve." Charlie's smile widened, and he threw out his arms. "It's perfect, don't you see? Poetic justice. Everyone will be outside, watching that stupid light parade and celebrating how safe and perfect everything is in Pleasant Creek. They won't be paying any attention to what's truly important, just like on the night of my parents' accident."

"What are you talking about?" Liz asked. "What are they not paying attention to?"

"Why are you trying to make sense out of this guy?" Rob shouted at her. "There's no point trying to understand someone like that. You're as crazy as he is!"

Charlie crossed the short distance to Rob in an instant and smacked the reporter in the side of the head. "You show some respect for the lady! She's had enough trouble from you."

Rob snarled at him. "You're insane. You should never have been placed in a group home. You belonged in a mental institution."

Charlie snatched a roll of duct tape from his coat pocket and slapped a piece over the reporter's mouth. "That should make everything nicer for all of us." He walked casually back over to the kerosene heater and warmed his hands.

"Fire is an interesting thing. It gives light. It warms. It's transformative, in a way." He turned to look at Liz. "Don't you agree?"

"I'm not sure." A curious barn cat crept onto Liz's lap, startling her.

He nodded. "You're still afraid of me, so you don't feel you can be honest. But I know you see the transformative powers of fire. You're a smart woman. During the light parade, when everyone is looking at the candles and the lights, I'm going to use fire to transform this town. I'm going to burn it down."

Liz gasped, her hand flying to her mouth of its own accord.

She couldn't believe what she'd just heard. "Not everyone will be at the parade. People could be killed."

The storyteller shook his head. "I'll be careful. I've chosen my targets well. Don't worry. After it's all over, I'll let you go. And the reporter too." He turned then to look at Rob. "I'm afraid you won't have a home to go back to, though. Your house is already wired to go up." Charlie clapped his hands. "*Whoosh*—no more home. But you won't mind. As you said, a lot of people have hard times. You wouldn't expect any sympathy for that."

"Charlie, you can't do this." Liz pulled the cat close to her, instinctively seeking the comfort its warm body offered. "You're punishing people who had nothing to do with your parents' accident or what happened to you. Rob isn't that much older than you. He was a kid when it happened. What could he have done?"

"It's not what he could have done then." Charlie's voice climbed in volume. "It's what his kind keeps doing. They keep turning a blind eye to suffering. They keep being heartless. They keep ruining this town."

"And what about your kind?" Liz held up the cat, drawing his attention to it. "The kind who leaves a kitten out in the cold, in a box where it could die? The kind who gives a nice person like Naomi a dead mouse right in her bakery, a place that brings joy to so many? What kind of heart do *you* have, Charlie?"

He blinked. "I knew those two in the cheese shop would find the kitten."

Liz hugged the cat close to her again. "What if they hadn't? Or what if they'd failed the test? What if they had been heartless and the kitten had died?"

"Then it would be on them."

"But *you* put the animal in the box!" she shouted. "*You* took it from its mother and shoved it in a box, Charlie. You. *You* left a baby out in the cold."

Charlie shook his head hard. "No. No. No." He clapped his hands over his ears. "That's not what I'm doing."

"It's what you did," Liz said. "And what about the cat bones in my box? What did that cat do to you?"

He latched onto that. "I didn't kill that cat. I found it outside the barn. I think a coyote killed it. I just used it."

"Like you used that tiny kitten?" She strategically pulled the conversation back to something that he couldn't defend. "Like you made it suffer in the cold? You treated it in exactly the same way you say the town treated you, Charlie—heartlessly."

"I'm not going to listen to any more of this." Charlie radiated agitation. "I wasn't going to tie you up like the reporter, but now I don't know. I don't know if you're the person I thought you were." He pulled the tape back out of his pocket and held it up, watching Liz. He seemed to enjoy the fear she knew must be on her face.

I cannot let him tie me up. If he did that, there would be no one to keep him from following through on his plan to burn down people's homes on Christmas Eve. And there was no certainty that she and Rob would survive either. In her fear, Liz hugged the cat tighter. She winced as it sank claws into her arm in annoyance at her tight grip.

Cat claws hurt. The realization bloomed like fireworks in her mind. *Cat claws* hurt!

Apparently, Charlie had had enough because he moved toward her with the tape. Liz stood slowly, holding the cat close.

"Don't make this more painful than it has to be," he said.

"No," she agreed. "I only want it to be exactly as painful as it has to be." Then she threw the barn cat right into his face. The surprised feline yowled its displeasure at the rough handling and scrambled for a grip, claws out.

Unfortunately for Charlie, the cat found its grip on his face. He bellowed as the cat's claws drew blood across his nose and cheeks.

As Charlie grappled with the cat, Liz ran for the door. She didn't want to abandon the reporter, but she doubted the cat would keep Charlie busy for long.

She underestimated the power of a truly angry cat.

The storyteller had been instinctively walking backward to get away from the pain, grabbing at the cat. However, the cat was equally focused on not being grabbed, so their struggle continued. Charlie's blind stagger brought him up against the kerosene heater, and he knocked it over, spilling oil and fire across the barn floor. The flames were out of control in seconds.

Charlie finally managed to fling the cat off his face and then dashed for the barn door. The cats fled as well. Liz changed directions and ran back to free Rob, who was making frantic sounds from behind his gag. She yanked the knife from the beam where Charlie had thrown it and cut the reporter free. Rob tried to stand, but doubled over, coughing at the smoke that filled the barn.

Wheezing along with him, Liz pulled up her scarf to cover her nose and mouth. "We have to get out of here," she choked out. She pulled Rob to his feet and dragged him a few steps even as he hunched over, his lungs full of smoke.

Finally, he straightened and looked around frantically. "Where is the door?"

Liz pointed with the knife. "That way."

"Where the fire is now?"

He had a point. The fire had totally cut them off. There was no escape.

21

Coughing hard, Liz looked around desperately. She began pulling Rob toward the section of barn where the smoke seemed less thick and she could still see the wall.

Rob resisted. "There's no door that way."

"This place is old. Maybe we can use the knife to get through the wall."

"You want to cut through a barn wall with a knife?" The reporter managed to convey scorn while still coughing and gasping for breath.

Liz let go of him and headed toward the clear wall. Rob could follow her or find his own way. She'd gotten him loose, but she wasn't going to waste time arguing with him.

When she reached the back wall, she heard voices and pressed her ear to one of the cracks between the wall boards.

"Liz?" It was Jackson, calling her name.

"Jackson!" she shouted through the crack. "Jackson, I'm here!"

"Liz!" Jackson yelled. "We can't get through the doors because of the fire. Where exactly are you?"

Liz shoved the knife blade into the crack. "Can you see the knife? That's where I am." Then, a coughing fit hit her and she doubled over.

"Move away from the wall as much as you can. I'm coming through."

Coming through? Liz backed away as much as she dared with the blasting heat of the fire behind her. She was surprised when the newspaperman staggered up beside her, coughing into a rag.

"What are you doing?" Rob asked.

"Not me. Jackson."

A thundering blow hit the outside of the barn. Liz saw cracks form along many of the wall boards. She heard an engine, and the building shook with another blow. This time, some of the planks broke clean through.

In moments, hands reached through the gaps, jerking at the broken boards. Liz and Rob scrambled to help, pulling at the split pieces of wood from their side of the wall. Soon, they had a hole big enough to crawl through. They were safe.

Jackson grabbed Liz by the upper arms and looked into her face, his expression frantic with worry. "Are you all right?"

She nodded, erupting into a coughing fit while Jackson pulled her farther from the still-burning ruin of the barn.

"The fire department is on the way," Jackson said.

"Charlie Newman." Liz choked out the name between coughs. "You have to stop him."

"He's already in custody." Jackson patted her back. "The chief grabbed him when he came running out of the barn door with his coat on fire. Unfortunately, the flames were too strong for us to get in."

"But how did you know where to find us? About Charlie?"

"Marty."

Liz blinked with surprise. "The woman from the newspaper office?"

Jackson nodded. "She called me. It seems she was more worried about Rob than she let on. After we left Rob's office, she went through his notes and found concerning information about Charlie. She was able to confirm that your storyteller was staying at the old motel on the edge of town. We found notes in his motel room that led us straight to this barn."

"Wait, how did you get inside Charlie's roo—?"

"Let's just say it helps to know the right people." Jackson smiled.

"I'm so thankful you got us out." Liz turned around to look at the barn and saw Jackson's beloved old pickup, its hood mangled and the bumper hanging by a thread. Jackson had backed it up and parked it a safe distance from the smoking barn, but its damage was aligned with the hole she had just crawled through. As she watched several of the barn cats gather around the wheels of the battered truck, she furrowed her brow. "You drove into the wall?"

"I could tell it wasn't very strong. And we had to get you out."

"Will your truck be okay?"

Jackson gaped at her. "I don't care about the truck."

Liz smiled. "And Charlie thought Pleasant Creek was heartless. He didn't know you."

Jackson looked at her quizzically. "I think we have a lot of catching up to do."

She nodded. "You have no idea. Let's just say we're on our way to a much merrier Christmas now."

The next few hours were a blur of questions and more poking and prodding than Liz would normally enjoy. Jackson had insisted that the official police interview wait until after Liz and Rob had been taken to the hospital to be checked out. The chief trailed them down the hospital corridors, though, ready to pepper them with his most pressing questions at the first opportunity.

Once Liz and Rob were examined and declared relatively healthy, the chief escorted them to a quiet waiting room with Jackson in tow.

"I just need to get the crucial details," the chief told them. "Then you can all head home."

Liz's throat felt raw from the smoke, so she was more than happy to let Rob do the talking, adding commentary only when the reporter's answers seemed too overblown or self-aggrandizing.

"I recognized the photos of his parents the second I saw them," Rob said. "I'd seen the guy around, and I'm good with faces. I caught up with him at the motel at the edge of town. He was making one of those packages. He'd even shoved a cat into it."

The chief nodded. "We saw it. He left it at Amish Cheese and More."

Rob shrugged. "He didn't tell me where he was taking it. He just jumped on me. I could have taken him, but I wasn't expecting him to go all crazy on me."

"You're lucky to be alive," Jackson said. "I hope you've thanked Liz."

Rob grinned at her, his teeth very white against the soot that still covered most of his face. "Yeah, thanks for getting me the story of the century. I hope this one gets me out of this town once and for all."

"I hope it does too." Liz's words were soft, but her meaning was fairly clear.

By the time Jackson drove her home in his poor, abused truck, Liz was exhausted. As he pulled up in front of the inn, she realized she had totally missed the social hour. She groaned. She'd missed the cookie swap as well.

"Is something the matter?" Jackson asked.

"Just thinking about the commitments I missed."

He smiled at her. "Once you show your face in there, I expect they'll understand and all will be forgiven."

Liz raised a hand to touch her cheek. Her skin felt dry, and her fingers came away with inky smudges. She thought of how soot-covered the reporter had been. Was she in a similar state? Liz tilted down the sunshade to inspect her reflection in the mirror. Her skin wasn't nearly as filthy as Rob's had been, but there were plenty of dark streaks. "Why didn't you tell me I'm such a mess?"

"I think you look fantastic."

Liz gave him a wry smirk. "Sure. All this time I've been wasting money on makeup when I look so good in soot."

He laughed. "You look alive. And that's wonderful to me."

"Well, I'd better go in and face the music with my guests." Liz sighed. "I definitely haven't shown them a very magical Christmas. I brought a storyteller into their midst who was secretly planning to burn down the whole town. How are they going to forgive me for that?"

"You saved Pleasant Creek," Jackson reminded her. "You saved Christmas. And you probably saved Rob's life. I think people are going to be inclined to cut you some slack."

"I hope so."

Jackson put his hand on the door handle, clearly intending to come around and help her out of the truck.

"That's all right." She opened her door on her own. "I can get inside by myself. You need to get home too. I'm not the only one who had a hard day."

"Are you sure?"

Liz nodded. "I'll see you tomorrow night for the light parade?"

"I wouldn't miss it." His eyes and smile radiated with his signature warmth.

She climbed out of the old pickup, wincing slightly as she saw the crumpled front bumper again. Then she walked glumly up to the inn and through the front door.

She was immediately engulfed in a hug. Sadie grasped her so tightly, Liz thought she felt her ribs creak.

"Don't you *ever* scare us like that again!" Sadie gave one final squeeze and then released her into Mary Ann's waiting arms.

"I'll try not to." Moving away from Mary Ann and further into the foyer, Liz looked around and saw the Sheltons standing in the doorway that led into the sitting room. The couple smiled at her, as did the twin sisters, who marched over and peered up at Liz.

"You look as if you've had a rough day," Gina said. "You should come in and sit down."

"And have a cookie," Lois added.

"Oh, the cookies." Liz looked back at Sadie and Mary Ann. "I missed the cookie swap. I'm so sorry."

"Not at all." Mary Ann waved her hands dismissively. "We found almost a whole tray of your chocolate bars from last night, so we put those in the swap. Then we saved your part of the exchange and shared them tonight for cookies and conversation."

Liz blinked with damp eyes. "Thank you. I should have known you two would save the day."

Vivian walked in with a cookie in her hand. "Speaking of saving the day, Sadie said you were off rescuing the town."

Liz gave her friend a questioning look, and Sadie explained. "Jackson called while the doctor was examining you. He knew we'd worry."

Liz smiled. Jackson was thoughtful that way.

"He painted you as quite the hero." Sadie beamed. "We want to hear all about it." She looked over Liz's soot-smeared clothes. "But maybe that can wait until later."

"If you don't mind." Liz made a futile attempt to smooth her hair. "I would love a shower."

Before Liz could limp out of the room, she heard the front door open behind her. She smiled as she turned, thinking that Jackson hadn't been willing to leave her to face the music alone.

To her utter shock, the man standing in the door wasn't Jackson.

Tears filled Liz's eyes as she groped for something to say.

The handsome young man brushed at his short hair with one hand, the other holding a large military green duffel he dropped on the floor. "Wouldn't you know, I barely get here and it starts to snow."

"Steve?" Liz whispered.

He grinned at her, but then his gaze swept from the top of her head to her feet. "Mom? What have you been doing? You look like Santa after a trip down the chimney."

That unfroze Liz's joints, and she ran across the room and flung herself at her godson. "You're home!"

He returned her hug with equal enthusiasm. "My change of plans got changed again. Is there room for one more at the inn?"

"There's always, *always* room at this inn for you," Liz said, her voice thick with tears of joy.

Suddenly, it looked like it might just be the merriest Christmas ever after all.

Learn more about Annie's fiction books at

AnniesFiction.com

- Access your e-books
- Discover exciting new series
- Read sample chapters
- Watch video book trailers
- Share your feedback

We've designed the Annie's Fiction website especially for you!

Plus, manage your account online!

- Check your account status
- Make payments online
- Update your address

ANNIE'S ATTIC
MYSTERIES®

CREATIVE WOMAN
MYSTERIES®

Annie's
Quilted
Mysteries™

Annie's
Mysteries

Unraveled™

ANNIE'S
SECRETS
of the QUILT™

AMISH
INN
MYSTERIES™

Visit us at AnniesFiction.com